KU-637-611

# JEWEL IN HIS CROWN

**'If you are not prepared to consider a normal marriage what are you suggesting?'**

'A total fake,' Ruby replied without hesitation, a hint of amusement lighting her unusually serious eyes. 'I marry you, and we make occasional public appearances together to satisfy expectations, but we're just pretending to be an ordinary married couple.'

The Prince concealed his surprise and mastered his expression, lest he make the mistake of revealing that inflicting such a massive deception on so many people would be abhorrent to his principles. 'A platonic arrangement?'

Ruby nodded with enthusiasm. 'No offence intended, but I'm really not into sex.'

*I'm really not into sex*, she had confided—and, like any man, he was intrigued. Since she could not make such an announcement and still be an innocent, he could only assume that she had suffered from the attentions of at least one clumsy lover. Raja surveyed her with a gleam of sensual speculation in his dark eyes. Far from being an amateur in the same field, he was convinced that, given the right opportunity, he could change her mind on that score…

**Lynne Graham** was born in Northern Ireland and has been a keen Mills & Boon® reader since her teens. She is very happily married, with an understanding husband who has learned to cook since she started to write! Her five children keep her on her toes. She has a very large dog, which knocks everything over, a very small terrier, which barks a lot, and two cats. When time allows, Lynne is a keen gardener.

**Recent titles by the same author:**

BRIDE FOR REAL *(The Volakis Vow)*
THE MARRIAGE BETRAYAL *(The Volakis Vow)*

**Did you know these are also available as eBooks?**
**Visit www.millsandboon.co.uk**

# JEWEL IN HIS CROWN

BY

LYNNE GRAHAM

All the characters in this book have no existence outside the imagination of the author, and have no relation whatsoever to anyone bearing the same name or names. They are not even distantly inspired by any individual known or unknown to the author, and all the incidents are pure invention.

All Rights Reserved including the right of reproduction in whole or in part in any form. This edition is published by arrangement with Harlequin Enterprises II BV/S.à.r.l. The text of this publication or any part thereof may not be reproduced or transmitted in any form or by any means, electronic or mechanical, including photocopying, recording, storage in an information retrieval system, or otherwise, without the written permission of the publisher.

® and TM are trademarks owned and used by the trademark owner and/or its licensee. Trademarks marked with ® are registered with the United Kingdom Patent Office and/or the Office for Harmonisation in the Internal Market and in other countries.

First published in Great Britain 2011
by Mills & Boon, an imprint of Harlequin (UK) Limited.
Harlequin (UK) Limited, Eton House, 18-24 Paradise Road,
Richmond, Surrey TW9 1SR

© Lynne Graham 2011

ISBN: 978 0 263 22127 5

MORAY COUNCIL
LIBRARIES &
INFO.SERVICES

20 33 21 43

Askews & Holts

RF RF

Harlequin (UK) policy is to use papers that are natural, renewable and [illegible] made from wood grown in sustainable forests. The logging and manufacturing process conform to the legal environmental regulations of the country of origin.

Printed and bound in Great Britain
by CPI Antony Rowe, Chippenham, Wiltshire

# CHAPTER ONE

THE beautiful brunette lay in the tangled bed sheets watching her lover get dressed. Prince Raja al-Somari had black hair and exotic dark golden eyes. Exceptionally handsome, he was pure leashed power, muscle and magnetic attraction. He was also a wild force of nature in bed, she reflected with a languorous look of sensual satisfaction on her face.

As his mistress, Chloe, one of the world's top fashion models, certainly had no complaints. But then Chloe was excessively fond of rich men, money and fabulous jewellery. Her prince from the oil-rich country of Najar in the Persian Gulf was staggeringly wealthy and he delivered on every count, so naturally she didn't want to lose him. When a plane crash had killed the bride in the arranged marriage being planned for Raja, Chloe had breathed a secret sigh of relief for such an alliance could well lead to the end of the most profitable relationship she had ever had. And even if another arranged marriage lurked on the horizon, Chloe was determined to hold onto her lover.

Raja watched Chloe finger the glittering new diamond bracelet encircling one slender wrist as if it were a talisman and his mouth quirked at her predictability. Although the demands of his position had made it difficult for him to see her in recent months, Chloe had subjected him to neither tantrums nor tears. Like most Western women he had met since his university days in England, she was as easy to placate as a child with a shiny new toy. In return for the complete discretion he demanded from his lovers, he was extremely generous but he never thought about his bed partners when he was away from them. Sex might be a necessity to a man of his appetites, but it was also simply an amusement and an escape from the weight of responsibility he carried. As acting Regent and ruler of conservative Najar, he could not openly enjoy a sex life without causing offence.

Furthermore, Raja was always aware that he had much more important issues to worry about. The recent appalling plane crash had devastated the people of Najar and its neighbour and former enemy, Ashur. The future of both countries stood on the edge of catastrophe. For seven years war had raged between oil-rich Najar and poverty stricken Ashur and when peace had finally been brokered by the Scandinavian state leading the talks, the two countries had added a more personal cultural twist to the agreement before they were satisfied that the peace would hold firm. That twist had been an arranged marriage between the two royal families and joint rulership that would ultimately unite Najar with Ashur. Having spent most of his adult life as a businessman before serving his country, Raja had accepted that he had to marry Princess Bariah of Ashur.

That she was a widow well into her thirties while he was still in his twenties he had accepted as his royal duty to put the needs of his country first. And his country and his people did desperately *need* a fresh blueprint for a lasting peace.

Unfortunately for all concerned, a tragedy had lurked in the wings of the peace accord. A fortnight earlier, Bariah and her parents had died in a plane crash. Shorn of its entire ruling family in one fell swoop, Ashur was in deep crisis and the court officials were searching frantically through the Shakarian family tree for a suitable heir to the throne who could take Bariah's place as Raja's bride and consort.

His mobile phone buzzed and he lifted it.

'You have to come home,' his younger brother Haroun told him heavily. 'Wajid Sulieman, the Ashuri court advisor, is already on his way here. According to his aide, he is very excited so I expect that means they've found another bride for you.'

It was the news that Raja had been waiting for, the news that honour demanded he hope for, but he still had to fight the crushing sensation of a rock settling on his chest to shorten his breathing. 'We must hope for the best—'

'The best would be if they *couldn't* find anyone else to marry you!' his youthful sibling opined without hesitation. 'Why are you letting yourself be forced into an arranged marriage? Are we still living in the Dark Ages?'

Raja's lean bronzed features were as impassive as he had learned to make them in the presence of others.

He rarely spoke without consideration. His wheelchair-bound father had taught him everything he knew about kingship. 'It is necessary that I do this.'

'Trouble?' Chloe asked, blue eyes bright with curiosity as Raja set down the phone and lifted his shirt.

'I have to leave immediately.'

Chloe scrambled out of bed and pressed her lithe pale body to his. 'But we were going out tonight,' she protested, looking up at him with wide, wounded eyes while being careful to look and sound hurt and disappointed rather than accusing, for there was very little Chloe didn't know about keeping a man happy.

'I'll make up for it on my next visit,' Raja promised, setting her to one side to resume dressing.

He was trying not to wonder *who* the Ashuri representatives had found for him to marry. What did the woman's identity matter? Hopefully she would be reasonably attractive. That was the most he could hope for. Anything more would be icing on the cake. He suppressed the thought that he was as imprisoned by his royal birth as an animal in a trap. Such reflections were unnecessarily dramatic and in no way productive.

His private jet whisked him back to Najar within hours and his brother was waiting in the limo that met him at the airport.

'I wouldn't marry a stranger!' Haroun told him heatedly.

'I do it gladly for you.' Raja was grateful that his kid brother had no such future sacrifice to fear. 'Right now, after a long period of instability, tradition is exactly what the people in both countries long to have back—'

'The Ashuris are broke. Their country is in ruins. Why don't you offer them a portion of our oil revenues instead?'

'Haroun!' Raja censured. 'Watch your mouth. Until we find a feasible framework for this peace agreement we all need to practise great diplomacy.'

'Since when has the truth been a hanging offence?' Haroun argued. 'We won the war yet you're being bartered off to a bunch of boundary thieves, who were still herding sheep when our great-great-grandfather, Rashid, was a king!'

Conscious that many Najaris would agree with his sibling, for the war had sown deep enmity and prejudice between the people of both countries, Raja merely dealt the younger man an impatient appraisal. 'I expect a more balanced outlook from a young man as well educated as you are.'

At the royal palace, the grey-haired and excessively precise Ashuri court advisor awaited Raja's arrival with an assistant and both men were, indeed, wreathed in smiles.

'My apologies if our timing has proved inconvenient, Your Royal Highness. Thank you for seeing us at such short notice.' Bowing very low, Wajid wasted no time in making small talk. A man on a mission, he spread open a file on the polished table between them. 'We have discovered that the only legal and marriageable female heir to the Ashuri throne is the daughter of the late King Anwar and a British citizen—'

'A British citizen?' Haroun repeated, intrigued.

'Anwar was ruler before Princess Bariah's father, King Tamim, wasn't he?'

'He was Tamim's elder brother. I recall that King Anwar made more than one marriage,' Raja remarked. 'Who was the lady's mother?'

The older man's mouth compressed. 'His first wife was an Englishwoman. The alliance was brief and she returned with the child to England after the divorce.'

'And what age is Anwar's daughter now?' Haroun was full of lively curiosity.

'Twenty-one years old. She has never been married.'

'Half English,' Prince Raja mused. 'And still very young. Of good character?'

Wajid stiffened. 'Of course.'

Raja was not so easily impressed. In his experience women who coveted the attentions of a prince were only looking for a good time and something sparkly to sweeten the deal. 'Why did King Anwar divorce her mother?'

'She was unable to have more children. It was a love match and short-lived,' the older man commented with a scornful compression of his lips. 'The king had two sons with his second wife, both of whom were killed during the war.'

Although Wajid was repeating information he was already well acquainted with, Raja dipped his head in respectful acknowledgement for a generation of young men had been decimated by the conflict that had raged for so long. As far as he was concerned if his marriage could persuade bitter enemies to live together in peace, it was a small sacrifice in comparison to the endless funerals he had once been forced to attend.

'The name of Anwar's daughter?'

'The princess's name is Ruby. As her mother chose to leave Ashur, the royal family took no further interest in either mother or daughter. Unfortunately Princess Ruby has had no training or preparation for a royal role.'

Raja frowned. 'In which case she would find the lifestyle and the expectations very challenging.'

'The princess is young enough to learn quickly.' The court advisor rubbed his hands together with unfeigned enthusiasm. 'Our advisors believe she can be easily moulded.'

'Have you a photograph to show my brother?' Haroun questioned eagerly.

Wajid leafed through the file and extracted a small photo. 'I'm afraid this is several years old but the most recent photograph we have.'

Raja studied the slender blonde in the miniskirt and tee shirt, captured outside the Ashuri cathedral in their capital city. It was a tourist snap and the girl still had the legginess and slightly chubby and unformed features of adolescence. Her pale colouring was very unusual in his culture and that long blonde hair was exceptionally attractive and he immediately felt guilty for that shallow reflection with his former fiancée, Bariah, so recently laid to rest. But in truth he had only met Bariah briefly on one formal occasion and she had remained a stranger to him.

Less guarded than his elder brother, Haroun studied

Princess Ruby and loosed a long low whistle of boyish approval.

'That is enough,' Raja rebuked the younger man in exasperation. 'When can I hope to meet her?'

'As soon as we can arrange it, Your Royal Highness.' Not displeased by the compliment entailed in Haroun's whistle of admiration, Wajid beamed, relieved by Raja's practical response to the offer of another bride. Not for the first time, Wajid felt that Prince Raja would be a king he could do business with. The Najari regent accepted his responsibilities without fuss and if there was one thing he knew inside out, it was *how* to be royal. A young woman blessed with his support and guidance would soon learn the ropes.

'*Please,* Ruby,' Steve pleaded, gripping Ruby's small waist with possessive hands.

'No!' Ruby told her boyfriend without hesitation. She pushed his hands from below her sweater. Although it didn't appear to bother him she felt foolish grappling with him in broad daylight in a car parked in the shadiest corner of the pub car park.

Steve dealt her a sulky look of resentment before finally retreating back into the driver's seat. Ruby, with her big brown eyes, blonde hair and fabulous figure, was a trophy and he was the envy of all his friends, but when she dug her heels in, she was as immovable as a granite rock. 'Can I come over tonight?'

'I'm tired,' Ruby lied. 'I should get back to work. I don't want to be late.'

Steve dropped her back at the busy legal practice

where she was a receptionist. They lived in the same Yorkshire market town. A salesman in an estate agency, Steve worked across the street from her and he was fighting a last-ditch battle to persuade Ruby that sex was a desirable activity. She had wondered if Steve might be the one to change her mind on that score for she had initially thought him very attractive. He had the blond hair and blue eyes she had always admired in men, but his kisses were wet and his roving hands squeezed her as if she were a piece of ripening fruit for sale on a stall. Steve had taught her that a man could be good-looking without being sexy.

'You're ten minutes late, Ruby,' the office manager, a thin, bespectacled woman in her thirties, remarked sourly. 'You need to watch your timekeeping.'

Ruby apologised and got back to work, letting her mind drift to escape the boredom of the routine tasks that made up her working day. When she had first started working at Collins, Jones & Fowler, she had been eighteen years old, her mother had just died and she had badly needed a job. Her colleagues were all female and older and the middle-aged trio of solicitors they worked for were an equally uninteresting bunch. Conversations were about elderly parents, children and the evening meal, never gossip, fashion or men. Ruby enjoyed the familiar faces of the regular clients and the brief snatches of friendly chatter they exchanged with her but continually wished that life offered more variety and excitement.

In comparison, her late mother, Vanessa, had had more than a taste of excitement while she was still young enough to enjoy it, Ruby recalled affectionately. As a youthful catwalk model in London, Vanessa had caught the eye of an Arab prince, who had married her after a whirlwind romance. Ruby's birthplace was the country of Ashur in the Persian Gulf. Her father, Anwar, however, had chosen to take a second wife while still married to her mother and that had been the ignominious end of what Vanessa had afterwards referred to as her 'royal fling'. Vanessa had got a divorce and had returned to the UK with her child. In Ashur daughters were rarely valued as much as sons and Ruby's father had promptly chosen to forget her existence.

A year later, Vanessa, armed with a substantial payoff and very much on the rebound, had married Curtis Sommerton, a Yorkshire businessman. She had immediately begun calling her daughter by her second husband's surname in the belief that it would enable Ruby to forget the family that had rejected them. Meanwhile Curtis had sneakily run through her mother's financial nest egg and had deserted her once the money was spent. Heartbroken, Vanessa had grieved long and hard over that second betrayal of trust and had died of a premature heart attack soon afterwards.

'My mistake was letting myself get carried away with my feelings,' Vanessa had often told her daughter. 'Anwar promised me the moon and I bet he promised the other wife he took the moon, as well. The proof of the pudding is in the eating, my love. Don't go falling for sweet-talking womanisers like I did!'

Fiery and intelligent, Ruby was very practical and quick to spot anyone trying to take too much advantage of her good nature. She had loved her mother very much and preferred to remember Vanessa as a warm and loving woman, who was rather naive about men. Her stepfather, on the other hand, had been a total creep, whom Ruby had hated and feared. Vanessa had had touching faith in love and romance but, to date, life had only taught Ruby that what men seemed to want most was sex. Finer feelings like commitment, loyalty and romance were much harder to find or awaken. Like so many men before him, Steve had made Ruby feel grubby and she was determined not to go out with him again.

After work she walked home, to the tiny terraced house that she rented, for the second time that day. Her lunch breaks were always cut short by her need to go home and take her dog out for a quick walk but she didn't mind. Hermione, the light of Ruby's life, was a Jack Russell terrier, who adored Ruby and disliked men. Hermione had protected Ruby from her stepfather, Curtis, on more than one occasion. Creeping into Ruby's bedroom at night had been a very dangerous exercise with Hermione in residence.

Ruby shared the small house with her friend Stella Carter, who worked as a supermarket cashier. Now she was surprised to see an opulent BMW car complete with a driver parked outside her home and she had not even contrived to get her key into the front door before it shot abruptly open.

'Thank goodness, you're home!' Stella exclaimed, her round face flushed and uneasy. 'You've got visitors in the lounge…' she informed Ruby in a suitable whisper.

Ruby frowned. 'Who are they?'

'They're something to do with your father's family… No, not Curtis the perv, the *real* one!' That distinction was hissed into Ruby's ear.

Completely bewildered, Ruby went into the compact front room, which seemed uncomfortably full of people. A small grey-haired man beamed at her and bowed very low. The middle aged woman with him and the younger man followed suit, so that Ruby found herself staring in wonderment at three downbent heads.

'Your Royal Highness,' the older man breathed in a tone of reverent enthusiasm. 'May I say what a very great pleasure it is to meet you at last?'

'He's been going on about you being a princess ever since he arrived,' Stella told her worriedly out of the corner of her mouth.

'I'm not a princess. I'm not a royal anything,' Ruby declared with a frown of wryly amused discomfiture. 'What's this all about? Who are you?'

Wajid Sulieman introduced himself and his wife, Haniyah, and his assistant. 'I represent the interests of the Ashuri royal family and I am afraid I must first give you bad news.'

Striving to recall her manners and contain her impatience, Ruby asked her visitors to take a seat. Wajid informed her that her uncle, Tamim, his wife and his daughter, Bariah, had died in a plane crash over the desert three weeks earlier. The names rang a very vague bell of familiarity from Ruby's one and only visit to

Ashur when she was a schoolgirl of fourteen. 'My uncle was the king…' she said hesitantly, not even quite sure of that fact.

'And until a year ago your eldest brother was his heir,' Wajid completed.

Ruby's big brown eyes opened very wide in surprise. 'I have a brother?'

Wajid had the grace to flush at the level of her ignorance about her relatives. 'Your late father had two sons by his second wife.'

Ruby emitted a rueful laugh. 'So I have two half-brothers I never knew about. Do they know about me?'

Wajid looked grave. 'Once again it is my sad duty to inform you that your brothers died bravely as soldiers in Ashur's recent war with Najar.'

Stunned, Ruby struggled to speak. 'Oh…yes, I've read about the war in the newspapers. That's very sad about my brothers. They must've been very young, as well,' Ruby remarked uncertainly, feeling hopelessly out of her depth.

The Ashuri side of her family was a complete blank to Ruby. She had never met her father or his relations and knew virtually nothing about them. On her one and only visit to Ashur, her once powerful curiosity had been cured when her mother's attempt to claim a connection to the ruling family was heartily rejected. Vanessa had written in advance of their visit but there had been no reply. Her phone calls once they arrived in Ashur had also failed to win them an invitation to the palace. Indeed, Vanessa and her daughter had finally been humiliatingly turned away from the gates of the royal palace when her father's relatives had not deigned to meet their estranged British relatives. From that moment on Ruby had proudly suppressed her curiosity about the Ashuri portion of her genes.

'Your brothers were brave young men,' Wajid told her. 'They died fighting for their country.'

Ruby nodded with a respectful smile and thought sadly about the two younger brothers she had never got the chance to meet. Had they ever wondered what she was like? She suspected that royal protocol might well have divided them even if, unlike the rest of their family, they had had sufficient interest to want to get to know her.

'I share these tragedies with you so that you can understand that you are now the present heir to the throne of Ashur, Your Royal Highness.'

'I'm the heir?' Ruby laughed out loud in sheer disbelief. 'How is that possible? I'm a girl, for goodness' sake! And why do you keep on calling me Your Royal Highness as if I have a title?'

'Whether you use it or otherwise, you have carried the title of Princess since the day you were born,' Wajid asserted with confidence. 'It is your birthright as the daughter of a king.'

It all sounded very impressive but Ruby was well aware that in reality, Ashur was still picking up the pieces in the aftermath of the conflict. That such a country had fought a war with its wealthy neighbour over the oil fields on their disputed boundary was a testament to their dogged pride and determination in spite of the odds against them. Even so she had been hugely relieved when she heard on the news that the war was finally over.

She struggled to appear composed when she was actually shaken by the assurance that she had a legal right to call herself a princess and then her natural common sense reasserted its sway. Could there be anything more ridiculously inappropriate than a princess who worked as a humble receptionist and had to struggle to pay her rent most months? Even with few extras in her budget Ruby was invariably broke and she often did a weekend shift at Stella's supermarket to help make ends meet.

'There's no room for titles and such things in my life,' she said gently, reluctant to cause offence by being any more blunt. 'I'm a very ordinary girl.'

'But that is exactly what our people would like most about you. We are a country of ordinary hard-working people,' Wajid declared with ringing pride. 'You are the only heir to the throne of Ashur and you must take your rightful place.'

Ruby's soft pink lips parted in astonishment. 'Let me get this straight—you are asking me to come out to Ashur and live there as a princess?'

'Yes. That is why we are here, to make you aware of your position and to bring you home.' Wajid spread his arms expansively to emphasise his enthusiasm for the venture.

A good deal less expressive, Ruby tensed and shook her fair head in a quiet negative motion. 'Ashur is not my home. Nobody in the royal family has even seen me since I left the country as a baby. There has been no contact and no interest.'

The older man looked grave. 'That is true, but the tragedies that have almost wiped out the Shakarian family have ensured that everything has changed. You are now a very important person in Ashur, a princess, the daughter of a recent king and the niece of another, with a strong legal claim to the throne—'

'But I don't want to claim the throne, and in any case I do know enough about Ashur to know that women don't rule there,' Ruby cut in, her impatience growing, for she felt she was being fed a rather hypocritical official line that was a whitewash of the less palatable truth. 'I'm quite sure there is some man hovering in the wings ready to do the ruling in Ashur.'

The court advisor would have squirmed with dismay had he not possessed the carriage of a man with an iron bar welded to his short spine. Visibly, however, he stiffened even more. 'You are, of course, correct when you say that women do not rule in Ashur. Our country has long practised male preference primogeniture—'

'So I am really not quite as important as you would like to make out?' Ruby marvelled that he could ever have believed she might be so ignorant of the hereditary male role of kingship in Ashur. After all, hadn't her poor mother's marriage ended in tears and divorce thanks to those strict rules? Her father had taken another wife in a desperate attempt to have a son.

Placed in an awkward spot when he had least expected it, Wajid reddened and revised up his assumptions about the level of the princess's intelligence. 'I am sorry to contradict you but you are unquestionably a very important young woman in the eyes of our people. Without you there can be no King,' he admitted baldly.

'Excuse me?' Her fine brows were pleating. 'I'm sorry, I don't understand what you mean.'

Wajid hesitated. 'Ashur and Najar are to be united and jointly ruled by a marriage between the two royal families. That was integral to the peace terms that were agreed to at the end of the war.'

Ruby froze at that grudging explanation and resisted the urge to release an incredulous laugh, for she suddenly grasped what her true value was to this stern little man. They needed a princess to marry off, a princess who could claim to be in line to the throne of Ashur. And here she was young and single. Nothing personal or even complimentary as such in her selection, she reflected with a stab of resentment and regret. It did, however, make more sense to her that she was only finally being acknowledged in Ashur as a member of the royal family because there was nobody else more suitable available.

'I didn't know that arranged marriages still took place in Ashur.'

'Mainly within the royal family,' Wajid conceded grudgingly. 'Sometimes parents know their children better than their children know themselves.'

'Well, I no longer have parents to make that decision for me. In any case, *my* father never took the time to get to know me at all. I'm afraid you're wasting your time here, Mr Sulieman. I don't want to be a princess and I don't want to marry a stranger, either. I'm quite content with my life as it is.' Rising to her feet to indicate that she felt it was time that her visitors took their leave, Ruby felt sorry enough for the older man in his ignorance of contemporary Western values to offer him a look of sympathy. 'These days few young women would be attracted by an arrangement of that nature.'

Long after the limousine had disappeared from view Ruby and Stella sat discussing the visit.

'A princess?' Stella kept on repeating, studying the girl she had known from primary school with growing fascination. 'And you honestly didn't know?'

'I don't think they can have wanted Mum to know,' Ruby offered evenly. 'After the divorce my father and his family were happy for her to leave Ashur and from then on they preferred to pretend that she and I didn't exist.'

'I wonder what the guy they want you to marry is like,' Stella remarked, twirling her dark fringe with dreamy eyes, her imagination clearly caught.

'If he's anything like as callous as my father I'm not missing anything. My father was willing to break Mum's heart to have a son and no doubt the man they want me to marry would do *anything* to become King of Ashur—'

'The guy has to be from the other country, right?'

'Najar? Must be. Probably some ambitious poor relation of their royal family looking for a leg up the ladder,' Ruby contended with rich cynicism, her scorn unconcealed.

'I'm not sure I would have been so quick to send your visitors packing. I mean, if you leave the husband out of it, being a princess might have been very exciting.'

'There was nothing exciting about Ashur,' Ruby assured her friend with a guilty wince at still being bitter about the country that had rejected her, for she had recognised Wajid Sulieman's sincere love for his country and the news of that awful trail of family deaths had been sobering and had left her feeling sad.

After a normal weekend during which her impressions of that astounding visit from the court advisor faded a little, Ruby went back to work. She had met up with Steve briefly on the Saturday afternoon and had told him that their relationship was over. He had taken it badly and had texted her repeatedly since then, alternately asking for another chance and then truculently criticising her and demanding to know what was wrong with him. She began ignoring the texts, wishing she had never gone out with him in the first place. He was acting a bit obsessive for a man she had only dated for a few weeks.

'Men always go mad over you,' Stella had sighed enviously when the texts started coming through again at breakfast, which the girls snatched standing up in the tiny kitchen. 'I know Steve's being a nuisance but I wouldn't mind the attention.'

'That kind of attention you'd be welcome to,' Ruby declared without hesitation and she felt the same at work when her phone began buzzing before lunchtime with more messages, for she had nothing left to say to Steve.

A tall guy with luxuriant black hair strode through the door. There was something about him that immediately grabbed attention and Ruby found herself help-lessly staring. Maybe it was his clothes, which stood out in a town where decent suits were only seen at weddings and then usually hired. He wore a strikingly elegant dark business suit that would have looked right at home in a designer advertisement in an exclusive magazine. It was perfectly modelled on his tall, well-built frame and long powerful legs. His razor-edged cheekbones were perfectly chiselled too, and as for those eyes, deep set, dark as sloes and brooding. *Wow*, Ruby thought for the very first time in her life as she looked at a man....

# CHAPTER TWO

WHEN Prince Raja walked into the solicitor's office, Ruby was the first person he saw and indeed, in spite of the number of other people milling about the busy reception area, pretty much the *only* person he saw. The pretty schoolgirl in the holiday snap had grown into a strikingly beautiful woman with a tumbling mane of blonde hair, sparkling eyes and a soft, full mouth that put him in mind of a succulent peach.

'You are Ruby Shakarian?' the prince asked as a tall, even more powerfully built man came through the door behind him to station himself several feet away.

'I don't use that surname.' Ruby frowned, wondering how many more royal dignitaries she would have to deflect before they got the hint and dropped this ridiculous idea that she was a princess. 'Where did you get it from?'

'Wajid Sulieman gave it to me and asked me to speak to you on his behalf. Shakarian is your family name,' Raja pointed out with an irrefutable logic that set her small white teeth on edge.

'I'm at work right now and not in a position to speak to you.' But Ruby continued to study him covertly, absorbing the lush black lashes semi-screening those mesmerising eyes, the twin slashes of his well-marked ebony brows, the smooth olive-toned skin moulding his strong cheekbones and the faint dark shadow of stubble accentuating his strong jaw and wide, sensual lips. Her prolonged scrutiny only served to confirm her original assessment that he was a stunningly beautiful man. Her heart was hammering so hard inside her chest that she felt seriously short of breath. It was a reaction that thoroughly infuriated her, for Ruby had always prided herself on her armour-plated indifference around men and the role of admirer was new to her.

'Aren't you going for lunch yet?' one of her co-workers enquired, walking past her desk.

'We could have lunch,' Raja pronounced, pouncing on the idea with relief.

Since his private jet had wafted him to Yorkshire and the cool spring temperature that morning, Prince Raja had felt rather like an alien set down on a strange planet. He was not used to small towns and checking into a third-rate local hotel had not improved his mood. He was cold, he was on edge and he did not relish the task foisted on him.

'If you're connected to that Wajid guy, no thanks to lunch,' Ruby pronounced as she got to her feet and reached for her bag regardless because she always went home at lunchtime.

The impression created by her seemingly long legs in that photo had been deceptive, for she was much smaller than Raja had expected and the top of her head barely reached halfway up his chest. Startled by that difference and bemused by that hitch in his concentration, Raja frowned. 'Connected?' he queried, confused by her use of the word.

'If you want to talk about the same thing that Wajid did, I've already heard all I need to hear on that subject,' Ruby extended ruefully. 'I mean...' she leant purposefully closer, not wishing to be overheard, and her intonation was gently mocking '...do I look like a princess to you?'

'You look like a goddess,' the prince heard himself say, speaking his thoughts out loud in a manner that was most unusual for him. His jaw tensed, for he would have preferred not to admit that her dazzling oval face had reminded him of a poster of a film star he recalled from his time serving with the Najari armed forces.

'A goddess?' Equally taken aback, Ruby suddenly grinned, dimples adorning her rounded cheeks. 'Well, that's a new one. Not something any of the men I know would come up with anyway.'

In the face of that glorious smile, Raja's fluent English vocabulary seized up entirely. 'Lunch,' he pronounced again stiltedly.

On the brink of saying no, Ruby recognised Steve waiting outside the door and almost groaned out loud. She knew the one infallible way of shaking a man off was generally to let him see her in the company of another. 'Lunch,' Ruby agreed abruptly, and she planted a determined hand on Raja's sleeve as if to take control of the situation. 'But first I have to go home and take my dog out.'

Raja was taken aback by that sudden physical contact, for people were never so familiar in the presence of royalty, and his breath rasped between his lips. 'That is acceptable.'

'Who is that guy over there watching us?' Ruby asked in a suspicious whisper, long blonde hair brushing his shoulder and releasing a tide of perfume as fragrant as summer flowers into the air.

'One of my bodyguards.' Raja advanced with the relaxed attitude of a male who took a constant security presence entirely for granted. 'My car is waiting outside.'

The bodyguard went out first, looked to either side, almost bumping into Steve, and then spread the door wide again for their exit.

'Ruby?' Steve questioned, frowning at the tall dark male by her side as she emerged. 'Who is this guy? Where are you going with him?'

'I don't have anything more to say to you, Steve,' Ruby stated firmly.

'I have a right to ask who this guy is!' Steve snapped argumentatively, his face turning an angry red below his fair, floppy fringe.

'You have no rights over me at all,' Ruby told him in exasperation.

As Steve moved forward the prince made an almost infinitesimal signal with one hand and suddenly a big bodyguard was blocking the younger man's attempt to get closer to Ruby. At the same time the other bodyguard had whipped open the passenger door to a long sleek limousine.

'I can't possibly get into a car with a stranger,' Ruby

objected, trying not to stare at the sheer size and opulence of the car and its interior.

Raja was unaccustomed to meeting with such suspicious treatment and it off-balanced him for it was not what he had expected from her. In truth he had expected her to scramble eagerly into the limo and gush about the built-in bar while helping herself to his champagne like the usual women he dated. But if the angry lovelorn young man shouting Ruby's name was typical of the men she met perhaps she was sensible to be mistrustful of his sex.

'I live close by. I'll walk back home first and meet you there.' Ruby gave him her address and sped across the street at a smart pace, deliberately not turning her head or looking back when Steve called her name.

The prince watched her walk away briskly. The breeze blew back her hair in a glorious fan of golden strands and whipped pink into her pale cheeks. She had big eyes the colour of milk chocolate and the sort of lashes that graced cartoon characters in the films that Raja's youngest relatives loved to watch. A conspicuously feminine woman, she had a small waist and fine curves above and below it. Great legs, delicate at ankle and knee. He wondered if Steve had lain between those legs and the shock of that startlingly intimate thought sliced through Raja as the limo wafted him past and he got a last look at her. A woman with a face and body like that would make an arranged marriage tempting to any hot-blooded male, he told himself impatiently. And just at that moment Raja's blood was running very hot indeed and there was a heavy tightness at his groin that signified a rare loss of control for him.

Ruby took Hermione out on her lead and by the time she unlocked the front door again, with the little black and white dog trotting at her heels, the limousine was parked outside waiting for her. This time she noticed that as well as the bodyguard in the front passenger seat there was also a separate car evidently packed with bodyguards parked behind it. Why was so much security necessary? Who was this guy? For the first time it occurred to Ruby that this particular visitor had to be someone more important than Wajid Sulieman and his wife. Certainly he travelled in much greater style. Checking her watch then, she frowned. There really wasn't time for her to have lunch with anyone and she dug out her phone to ring work and ask if she could take an extended lunch hour. The office manager advanced grudging agreement only after she promised to catch up with her work by staying later that evening.

As she stood in the doorway, Hermione having retreated to her furry basket in the living room, the passenger door of the limo was opened by one of the bodyguards. Biting her full lower lip in confusion, Ruby finally pulled the door of her home closed behind her and crossed the pavement.

'I really do need to know who you are,' she spelt out tautly.

For the first time in more years than he cared to recall, Raja had the challenge of introducing himself.

'Raja and you're a prince?' she repeated blankly, his

complex surname leaving her head as soon as she heard the unfamiliar syllables. 'But *who* are you?'

His wide, sensual mouth quirked and he surrendered to the inevitable. 'I'm the man Wajid Sulieman wants you to marry.'

And so great was the surprise of that admission that Ruby got into the car and sat back without further comment. This gorgeous guy was the man they wanted her to marry? He bore no resemblance whatsoever to her vague imaginings.

'Obviously you're from the other country, Najar,' she specified, recovering her ready tongue. 'A member of their royal family?'

'I am acting Regent of Najar. My father, King Ahmed, suffered a serious stroke some years ago and is now an invalid. I carry out his role in public because he is no longer able to do so.'

Ruby grasped the fine distinction he was making. Although his father suffered from ill health the older man remained the power behind the throne, doubtless restricting his son's ability to make his own decisions. Was that why Raja was willing to marry a stranger? Was he eager to assume power in Ashur where he could rule without his father's interference? Ruby hated being so ignorant. But what did she know about the politics of power and influence within the two countries?

One thing was for sure, however, Raja was very far from being the poor and accommodating royal hanger-on she had envisaged. Entrapped by her growing curiosity, she stole a long sidewise glance at him, noting the curling density of his lush black lashes, the high sculpted cheekbones that gave his profile such definition, the stubborn set of his masculine jaw line. Young, no more than thirty years of age at most, she estimated. Young, extremely good-looking *and* rich if the car and the security presence were anything to go by, she reasoned, all of which made it even harder for her to understand why he would be willing to even consider an arranged marriage.

'Someone digs up a total stranger, who just happens to be a long-lost relative of the Shakarian family, and you're immediately willing to marry her?' she jibed.

'I have very good reasons for my compliance and that is why I was willing to fly here to speak to you personally,' Raja fielded with more than a hint of quelling ice in his deep, dark drawl and he waved a hand in a fluid gesture of emphasis that caught her attention. His movements were very graceful and yet amazingly masculine at the same time. He commanded her attention in a way she had never experienced before.

An involuntary flush at that reflection warmed Ruby's cheeks, for in general aggressively male men irritated her. Her stepfather had been just such a man, full of sports repartee, beer and sexist comments while he perved on her behind closed doors. 'Nothing you could say is likely to change my mind,' she warned Raja ruefully.

Unsettled by the effect he had on her and feeling inordinately like an insecure teenager, Ruby lowered her eyes defensively and her gaze fell on the male leg positioned nearest to hers. The fine, expensive material of his tailored trousers outlined the lean, muscular power of his thigh while the snug fit over the bulge at his crotch defined his male attributes. As soon as she realised where her attention had lodged she glanced hurriedly away, her face hot enough to fry eggs on and shock reverberating through her, for it was the very first time she had looked at a man as if he were solely a sex object. When she thought of how she hated men checking her out she could only feel embarrassed.

The prince took her to the town's only decent hotel for lunch. He attracted a good deal of attention there, particularly from women, Ruby registered with growing irritation. It didn't help that he walked across the busy dining room like the royal prince that he was, emanating a positive force field of sleek sophistication and assurance that set him apart from more ordinary mortals. Beside him she felt seriously underdressed in her plain skirt and raincoat. She just knew the other female diners were looking at her and wondering what such a magnificent male specimen was doing with her. The head waiter seated them in a quiet alcove where, mercifully, Ruby felt less on show and more at ease.

While they ate, and the food was excellent, Raja began to tell her about the war between Najar and Ashur and the current state of recovery in her birth country. The whole time he talked her attention was locked on him. It was as if they were the only two people left on the planet. He shifted a shapely hand and she wondered what it would feel like to have that hand touching her body. The surprise of the thought made her face flame. She absorbed the velvet nuances of his accented drawl and recognised that he had a beautiful speaking voice.

But worst of all when she met the steady glitter of his dark, reflective, midnight gaze she felt positively light-headed and her mouth ran dry.

'Ashur's entire infrastructure was ruined and unemployment and poverty are rising,' Raja spelt out. 'Ashur needs massive investment to rebuild the roads, hospitals and schools that have been destroyed. Najar will make that investment but only if you and I marry. Peace was agreed solely on the basis of a marriage that would eventually unite our two countries as one.'

Gulping down some water in an attempt to ground herself to planet earth again, Ruby was surprised by the will power she had to muster simply to drag her gaze from his darkly handsome features and she said in an almost defiant tone, 'That's completely crazy.'

The prince angled his proud dark head in a position that signified unapologetic disagreement. 'Far from it. It is at present the only effective route to reconciliation which can be undertaken without either country losing face.' As he made that statement his classic cheekbones were taut with tension, accentuating the smooth planes of the olive-tinted skin stretched over his superb bone structure.

'Obviously I can see that nobody with a brain would want the war to kick off again,' Ruby cut in ruefully, more shaken than she was prepared to admit by the serious nature of Ashur's plight. She had not appreciated how grave the problems might be and even though the ruling family of her birth country had refused to acknowledge her existence, she was ashamed of the level of her ignorance.

'Precisely, and that is where *our* role comes in,' Raja imparted smoothly. 'Ashur can only accept my country's economic intervention if it comes wrapped in the reassurance of a traditional royal marriage.'

Ruby nodded in comprehension, her expression carefully blank as she asked what was for her the obvious question. 'So what's going to happen when this marriage fails to take place?'

In the dragging silence that fell in receipt of that leading query, his brilliant dark eyes narrowed and his lean, strong face took on a forbidding aspect. 'As the marriage was an established element of the peace accord, many will argue that if no marriage takes place the agreement has broken down and hostilities could easily break out again. Our families are well respected. Given the right approach, we could act as a unifying force and our people would support us in that endeavour for the sake of a lasting peace.'

'And you're willing to sacrifice your own freedom for the sake of that peace?' Ruby asked, wearing a dubious expression.

'It is not a choice. It is a duty,' Raja pronounced with a fluid shift of his beautifully shaped fingers. He said more with his hands than with his tongue, Ruby decided, for that eloquent gesture encompassed his complete acceptance of a sacrifice he clearly saw as unavoidable.

Ruby surveyed him steadily before saying without hesitation, 'I think that's a load of nonsense. How can you be so accepting of your duty?'

Raja breathed in deep and slow before responding to

her challenge. 'As a member of the royal family I have led a privileged life and I was brought up to appreciate that what is best for my country should be my prime motivation.'

Unimpressed by that zealous statement, Ruby rolled her eyes in cynical dismissal. 'Well, I haven't led a privileged life and I'm afraid I don't have that kind of motivation to fall back on. I'm not sure I can believe that you do, either.'

Under rare attack for his conservative views and for the depth of his sincerity, Raja squared his broad shoulders, his lean, dark features setting hard. He was offended but determined to keep his emotions in check. He suspected that the real problem was that Ruby rarely thought before she spoke and he virtually never met with challenge or criticism. 'Meaning?'

'Did you fight in the war?' Ruby prompted suddenly.

'Yes.'

Ruby's appetite ebbed and she rested back in her chair, milk-chocolate eyes telegraphing her contempt in a look that her quarry was not accustomed to receiving.

His tough jaw line clenched. 'That is the reality of war.'

'And now you think you can buy your way out of that reality by marrying me and becoming a saviour where you were once the aggressor?' Ruby fired back with a curled lip as she pushed away her plate. 'Sorry, I have no intention of being a pawn in a power struggle or of helping you to come to terms with your conscience. I'd like to leave now.'

On a wave of angry frustration Raja studied her truculent little face, his glittering eyes hostile. 'You haven't listened to me—'

Confident of her own opinion, Ruby lifted her chin in direct challenge of that charge. 'On the contrary, I've listened and I've heard as much as I need to hear. I can't be the woman you want me to be. I'm not a princess and I have no desire to sacrifice myself for the people or the country that broke my mother's heart.'

At that melodramatic response, Raja only just resisted the urge to groan out loud. 'You're talking like a child.'

A red-hot flush ran up to the very roots of Ruby's pale hair. 'How dare you?' she ground out, outraged.

'I dare because I need you to think like an adult to deal with this dilemma. You may be prejudiced against the country where you were born but don't drag up old history as an excuse—'

'There's nothing old about the way I grew up without a father,' Ruby argued vehemently, starting to rise from her chair in tune with her rapidly rising temper. 'Or the fact that he married another woman while he was still married to my mum! If that's what you call prejudice then I'm not ashamed to own up to it!'

'Lower your voice and sit down!' the prince ground out in a biting undertone.

Ruby was so stunned by that command that she instinctively fell back into her seat and stared across the table at him with a shaken frown of disbelief that he could think he had the right to order her around. 'Don't speak to me like that—'

'Then calm down and think of those less fortunate than you are.'

'It still won't make me willing to marry a stranger, who would marry a dancing bear if he was asked!' Ruby shot back at him angrily.

'What on earth are you trying to suggest?' Raja demanded, dark eyes blazing like angry golden flames above them.

More than ready to tell him what she thought of him, Ruby tossed down her napkin with a positive flourish. 'Did you think that I would be too stupid to work out what you're really after?' she asked him sharply. 'You want the throne in Ashur and I'm the only way you have of getting it! Without me and a ring on my finger, you get nothing!'

Subjecting her to a stunned look of proud incredulity, Raja watched with even greater astonishment as Ruby plunged upright, abandoned their meal and stalked away, hair flying, narrow back rigid, skirt riding up on those slender shapely thighs. Had she no manners? No concept of restraint in public places? She actually believed that he *wanted* the throne in Ashur? Was that her idea of a joke? She had no grasp of realities whatsoever. He was the future hereditary ruler of one of the most sophisticated and rich countries in the Persian Gulf, he did not need to rule Ashur, as well.

A brisk walk of twenty minutes brought Ruby back to work. A little breathless and flustered after the time she had had to consider that fiery exchange over lunch, she was still trying to decide whether or not she had been unfair in her assessment of Prince Raja. Waiting on her desktop for her attention was a pile of work, however, and her head was already aching from the stress of the information he had dumped on her.

At spare moments during the afternoon that followed she mulled over what she had learned about her birth country's predicament. It was not her fault all that had happened between Ashur and Najar, was it? But if Raja was correct and the peace broke down over the reality that their marriage and therefore the planned unification of the two countries did not take place, how would she feel about things then? That was a much less straightforward question and Ruby resolved to do some Internet research that evening to settle the questions she needed answered.

While Stella was cooking a late dinner, Ruby lifted the laptop the two young women shared, let Hermione curl up by her feet and sought information on the recent events in Ashur. Unfortunately a good deal of what she discovered was distressing stuff. Her late father's country, Ashur, she slowly recognised, desperately needed help getting back on its feet and people everywhere were praying that the peace would hold. Reading a charity worker's blog about the rising number of homeless people and orphans, Ruby felt tears sting her eyes and she blinked them back hurriedly and went to eat her dinner without an appetite. She could tell herself that Ashur was nothing to do with her but she was learning that her gut reaction was not guided by intellect. The war might be over but there was a huge job of rebuilding to be done and not enough resources to pay for it.

In the meantime the people of Ashur were suffering. Could the future of an entire country and its people be resting on what she chose to do?

Sobered by that thought and the heavy responsibility that accompanied it, Ruby started to carefully consider her possible options. Stella ate and hurried out on a date. While Ruby was still deep in thought and tidying up the tiny kitchen, the doorbell buzzed. This time she was not surprised to find Najar's much-decorated fighter-pilot prince on her doorstep again, for even she was now prepared to admit that they still had stuff to talk about. The sheer, dark masculine beauty of his bronzed features still took her by storm though and mesmerised her into stunned stillness. Those lustrous eyes set between sooty lashes in that stunningly masculine face exerted a powerful magnetic pull. She felt a tug at the heart of her and a prickling surge of heat. Once again, dragging her attention from him was like trying to leap single-handed out of a swamp.

'You'd better come in—we have to talk,' she acknowledged in a brittle breathless aside, exasperated by the way he made her stare and turning on her heel with hot cheeks to leave him to follow her.

'It's rude in my culture to turn your back on a guest or on royalty,' Raja informed her almost carelessly.

With a sound of annoyance, Ruby whipped her blonde head around to study him with frowning brown eyes. 'We have bigger problems than my ignorance of etiquette!'

As the tall, powerful man entered the room in Ruby's wake Hermione peered out of her basket, beady, dark eyes full of suspicion. A low warning growl vibrated in the dog's throat.

'No!' Ruby told her pet firmly.

'You were expecting my visit,' Raja acknowledged, taking a seat at her invitation and striving not to notice the way her tight black leggings and shrunken tee hugged her pert, rounded curves at breast and hip. The fluffy pink bunny slippers she wore on her tiny feet, however, made him compress his handsome mouth. He did not want to be reminded of just how young and unprepared she was for the role being offered to her.

Ruby breathed in deep, fighting the arrowing slide of shameless awareness keeping her unnaturally tense as she took a seat opposite him. Even at rest, the intoxicating strength of his tall, long-limbed, muscular body was obvious and she was suddenly conscious that her nipples had tightened into hard bullet points. She sucked in another breath, desperate to regain her usual composure. 'Yes, I was expecting you.'

Raja did not break the silence when her voice faltered. He waited patiently for her to continue with a quality of confident cool and calm that she found fantastically sexy.

'It's best if I lay my cards on the table this time. First of all, I would never, *ever* be prepared to agree to a normal marriage with a stranger, so that option isn't even a possibility,' Ruby declared without apology, knowing that she needed to tell him that upfront. 'But if you genuinely believe that only our marriage could ensure peace for Ashur, I feel I have to consider some way of bringing that about that we can both live with.'

Approbation gleamed in Raja's dark gaze because he believed that she was finally beginning to see sense. He was also in the act of reflecting that he could contrive to live with her without any great problem. He pinned his attention to the stunning contours of her face while remaining painfully aware of the full soft, rounded curves of her unbound breasts outlined in thin cotton. Clear indentations in the fabric marked the pointed evidence of her nipples and the flame of nagging heat at his groin would not quit. Angry at his loss of concentration at so important a meeting, however, he compressed his wide, sensual mouth and willed his undisciplined body back under his control.

'I *do* believe that only our marriage can give our countries the hope of an enduring peace,' he admitted. 'But if you are not prepared to consider a normal marriage, what are you suggesting?'

'A total fake,' Ruby replied without hesitation, a hint of amusement lightening her unusually serious eyes. 'I marry you and we make occasional public appearances together to satisfy expectations but behind closed doors we're just pretending to be an ordinary married couple.'

The prince concealed his surprise and mastered his expression lest he make the mistake of revealing that inflicting such a massive deception on so many people would be abhorrent to his principles. 'A platonic arrangement?'

Ruby nodded with enthusiasm. 'No offence intended but I'm really not into sex—'

'With me? Or with anyone?' Raja could not resist demanding that she make that distinction.

'Anyone. It's nothing personal,' she hastened to assure a male who was taking it all very personally indeed. 'And it will also give you the perfect future excuse to divorce me.'

Hopelessly engaged in wondering what had happened to her to give her such a distaste for intimacy, Raja frowned in bewilderment. 'How?'

'Well, obviously there won't be a child. I'm not stupid, Raja. Obviously if we get married a son and heir is what everyone will be hoping for,' she pointed out wryly. 'But when there is no pregnancy and no child, you can use that as a very good reason to divorce me and then marry someone much more suitable.'

'It would not be that simple. I fully understand where you got this idea from though,' he imparted wryly. 'But while your father may have divorced your mother in such circumstances, there has never been a divorce within my family and our people and yours would be very much shocked and disturbed by such a development.'

Ruby shrugged a slight shoulder in disinterested dismissal of that possibility. 'There isn't going to be a *perfect* solution to our dilemma,' she told him impatiently. 'And I think that a fake marriage could well be as good as it gets. Take it or leave it, Raja.'

Raja almost laughed out loud at that impudent closing speech. What a child she still was! He could only begin to imagine how deeply offended the Ashuri people would be were he to divorce their princess while seeking to continue to rule their country. What she was suggesting was only a stopgap solution, not a permanent remedy to the dilemma.

'Well, that's one angle but not the only one,' Ruby continued ruefully. 'I have to be very blunt here…'

An unexpected grin slanted across Raja's beautifully moulded mouth, for in his opinion she had already been exceedingly frank. 'By all means, be blunt.'

'I would have to have equal billing in the ruling stakes,' she told him squarely. 'I can't see how you can be trusted to look out for the interests of both countries when you're from Najar. You would have an unfair advantage. I will only agree to marry you if I have as much of a say in all major decisions as you do.'

'That is a revolutionary idea and not without its merits,' Raja commented, striving not to picture Wajid Sulieman's shattered face when he learned that his princess was not, after all, prepared to be a powerless puppet on the throne. 'You should have that right but it will not be easy to convince the councils of old men, who act as the real government in our respective countries. In addition, you will surely concede that you know nothing about our culture—'

'But I can certainly learn,' Ruby broke in with stubborn determination. 'Well, those are my terms.'

'You won't negotiate?' the prince prompted.

'There is no room for negotiation.'

Raja was grimly amused by that uncompromising stance. In many ways it only emphasised her naivety. She assumed that she could break all the rules and remain untouched by the consequences yet she had no idea of what real life was like in her native country.

Without that knowledge she could not understand how much was at stake. He knew his own role too well to require advice on how to respond to her demands.

Royal life had taught him early that he did not have the luxury of personal choice. His primary duty was to persuade the princess to take up her official role in Ashur and to marry her, twin objectives that he was expected to achieve by using any and every means within his power. His father had made it clear that the need for peace must overrule every other consideration. Any natural reluctance to agree to a celibate marriage in a society where extramarital sex was regarded as a serious evil did not even weigh in the balance.

*I'm really not into sex*, she had confided and, like any man, he was intrigued. Since she could not make such an announcement and still be an innocent he could only assume that she had suffered from the attentions of at least one clumsy lover. Far from being an amateur in the same field, Raja surveyed her with a gleam of sensual speculation in his dark eyes. He was convinced that given the right opportunity he could change her mind on that score.

'Well, what do you think?' Ruby pressed edgily as she rose to her feet again.

'I will consider your proposition,' the prince conceded non-committally, springing upright to look down at her with hooded, dark eyes.

His ability to conceal his thoughts from his lean, dark features infuriated Ruby, who had always found the male sex fairly easy to read. For once she had not a clue what a man might be thinking and her ignorance intimidated and frustrated her. Like the truly stunning dark good looks that probably turned heads wherever he went, the prince's reticence was one of his most noticeable attributes. He had the skills of a natural-born diplomat, she conceded, grudgingly recognising how well equipped he was to deal with opposing viewpoints and sensitive political issues.

'I thought time was a real matter of concern,' Ruby could not help remarking, irritated by his silence.

A highly attractive grin slanted his wide sensual mouth. 'If you give me your phone number I will contact you later this evening with my answer.'

Ruby gave him that information and walked out to the front door. As she began to open it he rested a hand on her shoulder, staying her, and she glanced up from below her lashes, eyes questioning. Hermione growled. Raja ignored the animal, sliding his hand lightly down Ruby's arm and up again, his handsome head lowering, his proud gaze glittering as bright as diamonds from below the fringe of his dense black lashes. She stopped breathing, moving, even thinking, trapped in the humming silence while a buzz of excitement unlike anything she had ever experienced trailed along her nerve endings like a taunting touch.

His breath warmed her cheek and she focused on his strong sensual mouth, the surge of heat and warmth between her thighs going crazy. Desire was shooting through her veins like adrenalin and she didn't understand it, couldn't control it either, any more than she could defy the temptation to rest up against him, palms spread across his chest to absorb the muscular strength of his powerful frame and remain upright. Eyes wide, she stared up at him, trembling with anticipation and he did not disappoint her. On the passage to her mouth his lips grazed the pulse quivering in her neck and an almost violent shimmy of sensation shot down through her slight length. His hand sliding down to her waist to steady her, he circled her mouth with a kiss as hot as a blowtorch. The heat of his passion sent a shock wave of sexual response spiralling down straight into her pelvis.

Raja only lifted his head again when Hermione's noisy assault on his ankles became too violent to ignore. 'Call off your dog,' he urged her huskily.

Grateful for the excuse to move, Ruby wasted no time in capturing her snarling pet and depositing her back in the living room. Her hands were shaking. Nervous perspiration beaded her upper lip. Ruby was in serious shock from finally feeling what a man had never made her feel before. She was still light-headed from the experience, and her temper surged when she caught Raja studying her intently. Consumed by a sense of foolishness, she was afraid that he might have noticed that she was trembling and her condemnation was shrill. 'You had no right to touch me!'

His lustrous dark eyes glinted like rapier blades over her angry face. 'I had no right but I was very curious,' he countered with a studied insolence that pushed a tide of colour into her cheeks. 'And you were worth the risk.'

A moment later he was gone and she closed the door, only just resisting the urge to slam it noisily. She was still as wound up as a clock spring. Men didn't speak to Ruby in that condescending tone and they rarely, if ever, offered her provocation. Invariably they tried to please her and utilised every ploy from flattery to gifts to achieve that end. Raja, on the other hand, had subjected her to a cool measuring scrutiny and had remained resolutely unimpressed and in control while she fell apart and she could only hate him for that: *she* had shown weakness and susceptibility, he had not.

Her phone rang at eleven when she was getting ready for bed.

'It's Raja.' His dark drawl was very businesslike in tone and delivery. 'I hope you're prepared to move quickly on this as time is of the essence.'

Taut with strain and with her teeth gritted, for it was an effort to be polite to him with her pride still stinging from that kiss that she had failed to rebuff, Ruby said stiffly, 'That depends on whether or not you're prepared to stand by my terms.'

'You have my agreement. While I make arrangements for our marriage to take place here—'

'Like soon…*now*? And we're to get married *here*?' Ruby interrupted, unable to swallow back her astonishment.

'It would be safer and more straightforward if the deed were already done before you even set foot in Ashur because our respective representatives will very likely quarrel about the when and the where and the how of our wedding for months on end,' the prince informed her wryly. 'In those circumstances, staging a quiet ceremony here in the UK makes the most sense.'

Infuriatingly at home giving orders and impervious to her tart comments, Raja advised her to resign from her job immediately and start packing. Ruby stayed out of bed purely to tell Stella that she was getting married. Her friend was stunned and less moved than Ruby by stories of Ashur's current instability and economic hardship.

'You're not thinking about what you're doing,' Stella exclaimed, her pretty face troubled. 'You've let this prince talk you round. He made you feel bad but, let's face it, your life is here. What's your father's country got to do with you?'

Only forty-eight hours earlier, Ruby would have agreed with that sentiment. But matters were not so cut and dried now. Ashur's problems were no longer distant, impersonal issues and she could not ignore their claim on her conscience. In her mind the suffering there now bore the faces of the ordinary people whose lives had been ruined by the long conflict.

Ruby compressed her generous mouth. 'I just feel that if I can do something to help, I should do it. It won't be a proper marriage, for goodness' sake.'

'You might get over there and find out that the prince already has a wife,' Stella said with a curled lip.

'I don't think so. He wouldn't be here if I wasn't needed.'

Unaccustomed to Ruby being so serious, Stella pulled a face. 'Well, look what happened to your mother when she married a man from a different culture.'

'But Mum was in love while I would just be acting out a role. I won't get hurt the way she did. I'm not stuffed full of stupid romantic ideas,' Ruby declared, her chin coming up. 'I'm much tougher and I can look after myself.'

'I suppose you know yourself best,' Stella conceded, taken aback by Ruby's vehemence.

Ruby couldn't sleep that night. The idea of marrying Najar's Prince still felt unreal. She could have done without her friend's honest reminder that her mother's royal marriage had gone badly wrong. Although Ruby knew that she had absolutely no romantic interest in Raja and was therefore safe from being hurt or disappointed by him, she could not forget the heartbreak her mother had suffered when she had attempted to adapt to a very different way of life.

At the same time the haunting images Ruby had seen of the devastation in Ashur kept her awake until the early hours. The plight of her father's people was the only reason she was willing to agree to such a marriage, she reflected ruefully. Even though she was being driven by good intentions the prospect of marrying a prince and making her home in a strange land filled her to overflowing with doubts and insecurity.

In recent years she had often regretted the lack of excitement in her life, but now all of a sudden she was being confronted with the truth of that old adage: *Be careful of what you wish for....*

# CHAPTER THREE

THE saleswoman displayed a ghastly, shapeless plum-coloured suit that could only have pleased a woman who had lost interest in her appearance. Of course it was not the saleswoman's fault, Ruby reasoned in growing frustration; it was Raja's insistence on the outfit being 'very conservative and plain' that had encouraged the misunderstanding of what Ruby might be prepared to wear at her wedding.

'That's not me, that's really not my style!' Ruby declared with a grimace.

'Then choose something and quickly,' the prince urged in an impatient aside for he was not a patient shopper. 'Show some initiative!'

Raja did not understand why what she wore should matter so much. After all, even in her current outfit of faded jeans and a blue sweater she looked beautiful enough in his opinion to stop traffic. Luxuriant honey-blonde hair tumbled round her narrow shoulders. Denim moulded her curvy derrière and slim thighs, wool cupped the swell of her pouting breasts and emphasised her small waist. Even unadorned, she had buckets of utterly natural sex appeal. As he recognised the swelling heaviness of arousal at his groin his lean dark features clenched hard and he fixed his attention on the wall instead.

*Show some initiative?* Dull coins of aggravated red blossomed over Ruby's cheekbones and her sultry pink mouth compressed. Where did someone who had so far dismissed all her helpful suggestions get the nerve to taunt her with her lack of initiative? It was only an hour and a half since she had met her future husband at his hotel to sign the various forms that would enable them to get married in a civil ceremony and he was already getting on her nerves so much that she wanted to kill him! Or at the very least kick him! A high-ranking London diplomat had also attended that meeting to explain that a special licence was being advanced to facilitate their speedy marriage. Raja, she had learned, enjoyed diplomatic immunity. He was equally immune, she was discovering, to any sense of fashion or any appreciation of female superiority.

Stalking up to the rail of the town's most expensive boutique, Ruby began to leaf through it, eventually pulling a red suit out. 'I'll try this one on.'

The prince's beautifully shaped mouth curled. 'It is very bright.'

'You did say that a formal publicity photo would be taken and I don't want to vanish into the woodwork,' Ruby told him sweetly, big brown eyes wide with innocence but swiftly narrowing to stare intently at his glorious face. He was gorgeous. That fabulous bone structure and those dark deep-set eyes set below that slightly curly but ruthlessly cropped black hair took her breath away every time.

The saleswoman took the suit to hang it in a dressing room. With fluid grace Raja lifted his hand and let his thumb graze along the fullness of Ruby's luscious lower lip. His dark eyes glittered hot as coals as he felt that softness and remembered the sweet heady taste of that succulent mouth beneath his own. Tensing, Ruby dealt him a startled look, her lips tingling at his touch while alarm tugged at her nerves. As his hand dropped she moved closer and muttered in taut warning, 'This is business, just business between us.'

'Business,' the prince repeated, his accent scissoring round the label like a razor-sharp blade. Business was straightforward and Ruby Shakarian was anything but. He watched her sashay into the dressing room, little shoulders squared, hair bouncing, all cheeky attitude and surplus energy. He wanted to laugh but he had far too much tact. He didn't agree with her description. Business? No, he wanted to have sex with her. He wanted to have sex with her very, very much. He knew that and accepted it as a natural consequence of his male libido. Desire was a predictable response in a young and healthy man when he was with a beautiful woman. It was also a positive advantage in a royal marriage. Sex was sex, after all, little more than an entertaining means to an end when children were required. Finer feelings were neither required nor advisable. Been there, done that, Raja acknowledged in a bleak burst of recollection from the past. He had had his heart broken once and had sworn he would never put it up for a woman's target practice again.

Even so, once Ruby was his wife Raja had every intention of ensuring that the marriage followed a much more conventional path than she presently intended. Obviously he didn't want a divorce. A divorce would mean he had failed in his duty, failed his family and *failed* his very country. He breathed in deep and slow at that aggrieved acknowledgement, mentally tasting the bite of such a far-reaching failure and striving not to flinch from it. After all there was only so much that he *could* do. It was unfair that so much should rest on his ability to make a success of an arranged marriage but Raja al-Somari had long understood that life was rarely fair. The bottom line was that he and everyone who depended on them needed their prince and princess to build a relationship with a future. And a fake marriage could never achieve that objective.

Over the three days that followed Ruby was much too busy to get cold feet about the upheaval in her life. She resigned from her job without much regret and began packing, systematically working through all her possessions and discarding the clutter while Stella lamented her approaching departure and placed an ad in the local paper for a new housemate. The day before the wedding, Hermione, accompanied by her favourite squeaky toy and copious instructions regarding her care and diet, was collected to be transported out to Ashur in advance. The memory of her pet's frightened little eyes above her greying muzzle as she looked out through the barred door of her pet carrier kept her mistress awake that night.

The wedding was staged with the maximum possible discretion in a private room at the hotel with two diplomats acting as official witnesses. Accompanied only by Stella, Ruby arrived and took her place by Raja's side. His black hair displaying a glossy blue-black sheen below the lights, dark eyes brilliant shards of light between the thick fringe of his lashes, Raja looked impossibly handsome in a formal, dark pinstripe suit. When he met her appraisal he didn't smile and his lean bronzed features remained grave. She wondered what he was thinking. Not knowing annoyed her. Her heart was beating uncomfortably fast by the time that the middle-aged registrar began the short service. Raja slid a gold ring onto her finger and because it was too big she had to crook her finger to keep the ring from falling off. The poorly fitting ring struck her as an appropriate addition to a ceremony that, shorn of all bridal and emotional frills, left her feeling distinctly unmarried.

It was done, goal achieved, Raja reflected with considerable satisfaction. His bride had not succumbed to a last-minute change of heart as he had feared. He studied Ruby's delicately drawn profile with appreciation. She might look fragile as a wild flower but she had a core of steel, for she had given her word and although he had sensed her mounting tension and uncertainty she had defied his expectations and stuck to it.

One of the diplomats shook Ruby's hand and addressed her as 'Your Royal Highness', which felt seriously weird to her.

'I'm never ever going to be able to see you as a princess,' Stella confided with a giggle.

'Give Ruby time,' Raja remarked silkily.

Colour tinged Ruby's cheeks. 'I'm not going to change, Stella.'

'Of course you will,' the prince contradicted with unassailable confidence, escorting his bride over to a floral display on a table where the photographer awaited them. 'You're about to enter a different life and I believe you'll pick up the rules quickly. Smile.'

'Raja,' Ruby whispered sweetly, and as he inclined his arrogant, dark head down to hers she snapped, '*Don't* tell me what to do!'

'Petty,' he told her smoothly, his shrewd gaze encompassing the photographer within earshot.

And foolish as it was over so minor an exchange, Ruby's blood boiled in her veins. She hated that sensation of being ignorant and in the position that she was likely to do something wrong. Even more did she hate being bossed around and told what to do and Raja al-Somari rapped out commands to the manner born. No doubt she would make the occasional mistake but she was determined to learn even quicker than he expected for both their sakes.

Chin at a defiant angle, Ruby gave Stella a quick hug, promised to phone and climbed into the limousine to travel to the airport. She would have liked the chance to change into something more comfortable in which to travel but Raja had stopped her from doing so, advising her that while she was in her official capacity as a princess of Ashur and his wife she was on duty and had to embrace the conservative wardrobe. His wife, Ruby thought in a daze of disbelief, thinking back to the previous week when she had been kissing Steve in his car. How could her life have changed so much in so short a time?

But she comforted herself with the knowledge that she wasn't *really* his wife, she was only pretending. Boarding the unbelievably opulent private jet awaiting them and seeing the unconcealed curiosity in the eyes of the cabin staff, Ruby finally appreciated that pretending to be a princess married to Raja was likely to demand a fair degree of acting from her. Instead of kicking off her shoes and curling up in one of the cream leather seats in the cabin, she found herself sitting down sedately and striving for a dignified pose for the first time in her life.

Soon after take-off, Raja rose from his seat and settled a file down in front of her. 'I asked my staff to prepare this for you.' He flipped it open. 'It contains photos and names for the main members of the two royal households and various VIPs in both countries as well as other useful information—'

'Homework,' Ruby commented dulcetly. 'To think I thought I'd left that behind when I left school.'

'Careful preparation should make the transition a little easier for you.'

Ruby could not credit how many names and faces he expected her to memorise, and the lengthy sections encompassing history, geography and culture in both countries made distinctly heavy reading. After a light lunch was served, Ruby took a break and watched Raja working on his laptop, lean fingers deft and fast. Her husband? It still didn't feel credible. His black lashes shaded his eyes like silk fans and when he glanced at her with those dark deep-set eyes that gleamed like polished bronze, something tripped in her throat and strangled her breathing. He was drop-dead gorgeous and naturally she was staring. Any woman would, she told herself irritably. She didn't fancy him; she did *not*.

Raja left the main cabin to change and reappeared in a white, full-length, desert-style robe worn with a headdress bound with a black and gold cord.

'You look just like you're starring in an old black and white movie set in the desert,' she confided helplessly, totally taken aback by the transformation.

'That is not a comment I would repeat in Najar, where such a mode of dress is the norm,' Raja advised her drily. 'I do not flaunt a Western lifestyle at home.'

Embarrassment stirring red heat in her cheeks, Ruby dealt him a look of annoyance. 'Or a sense of humour.'

But in truth there was nothing funny about his appearance. He actually looked amazingly dignified and royal and shockingly handsome. Even so his statement that he did not follow a Western lifestyle sent an arrow of apprehension winging through her. What other surprises might lie in wait for her?

A few minutes later he warned her that the jet would be landing in Najar in thirty minutes. When she returned after freshening up he announced with the utmost casualness that they would be parting once the jet landed. She would be flying straight on to Ashur where he would join her later in the week.

Ruby was shattered by that unexpected news and her head swivelled, eyes filled with disbelief. 'You're leaving me to travel on alone to Ashur?'

'Only for thirty six hours at most. I'm afraid that I can't be in two places at once.'

'Even on what's supposed to be our wedding night?' Ruby launched at him.

The prince shut his laptop and shot her a veiled look as silky as melted honey and somehow that appraisal made her tummy perform acrobatics. 'Are you offering me one?'

The silence simmered like a kettle on the boil. Her cheeks washed with heat, Ruby scrambled to her feet. 'Of course, I'm not!'

'I thought not. So, what's the problem? The exact date of our marriage will not be publicly announced. Very few people will be aware that this is our wedding night.'

Ruby almost screamed. He was not that stupid. He was seriously not that stupid and his casual reaction to her criticism enraged her. She breathed in so deep and long she was vaguely surprised that her head didn't lift off her shoulders and float. 'You're asking me what the problem is? Is that a joke?'

Raja uncoiled from his seat with the fluid grace of a martial arts expert. Standing very straight and tall, broad shoulders hard as a blade, Raja rested cool eyes on her, for he was not accustomed to being shouted at and he was in no mood to become accustomed to the experience. 'Naturally I am not joking.'

'And you can't see anything wrong with dumping me with a bunch of strangers in a foreign country? I don't know anyone, don't speak the language, don't even know *how* to behave,' Ruby yelled back at him full volume, causing the steward entering the cabin with a trolley to hastily backtrack and close the door again. 'How can you abandon me like that?'

The prince gazed down at her with frowning dark eyes, exasperated by her ignorance. Clearly she had no concept of the extensive planning and detailed security arrangements that accompanied his every movement and that would soon apply equally to hers. Familiar as Raja was with the military precision of planning a royal schedule set in stone often months in advance, he saw no room for manoeuvre or a change of heart. 'Abandon you? How am I abandoning you?'

Made to feel as if she was being melodramatic, Ruby reddened and pursed her sultry mouth. 'You're supposed to be my husband.'

Taken aback by the reminder, Raja quirked an expressive ebony brow. 'But according to you we're only faking it.'

'Well, you're not faking it worth a damn!' Ruby condemned with furious bite, strands of hair shimmying round her flushed cheekbones, eyes accusing. 'A husband should be loyal and supportive. I don't know how to be a princess yet and if I make mistakes I'm likely to offend people. Hasn't that occurred to you? You can't leave me alone in a strange place. I don't know how to give these people what they expect and deserve and I was depending on you to tell me!'

Unprepared for his gutsy bride to reveal panic, Raja frowned, setting his features into a stern mask. 'Unfortunately arrangements are already in place for us to go our separate ways this afternoon. It is virtually impossible to make last-minute changes to that schedule. We're about to land in Najar, I'm expected home and you're flying on to Ashur by yourself.'

Suddenly mortified by the nerves that had got the better of her composure, Ruby screened her apprehensive gaze and said stiffly as she took her seat with determination again, 'Fine. Don't worry about it—I'm sure I'll manage. I'm used to being on my own.'

Ruby didn't speak another word. She was furious with herself for revealing her insecurity. What on earth had she expected from him? Support? When had she ever known a man to be supportive? Raja had his own priorities and they were not the same as hers. As he had reminded her, their marriage, their very relationship, was a fake. As, to be fair, she had requested. Her soft, full mouth curved down. Clearly if she wasn't sleeping with him she was on her own and that was nothing new....

## CHAPTER FOUR

THE instant Ruby stepped out of the plane the heat of the sun engulfed her in a powerful wave, dewing her upper lip with perspiration and giving the skin below her clothes a sticky feeling. In the distance an architectural triumph of an airport building glinted in the sun. A man bowed low in front of her and indicated a small plane about fifty yards away. Breathing in deep and slow to steady her nerves, Ruby followed him.

At the top of the steps and mere seconds in her wake, the prince came to a dead halt, rare indecision gripping him.

*'You're supposed to be my husband...loyal and supportive.'*

*'How can you abandon me?'*

His stubborn jaw line clenched. He gritted his teeth. He could not fault her expectations. Would he not expect similar consideration from her? He was also a very masculine guy and it went against the grain to ignore her plea for help. At a time when her role was still so new to her, even a temporary separation was a bad idea. Of course she was feeling overwhelmed and he was well aware that people would be only too willing to find fault when she made innocent mistakes. He strode down the steps, addressed the court official waiting to greet him and politely ignored the surprise, dismay and the sudden burst of speech that followed his declaration of a change of plan. All the signs were that the little plane parked on the asphalt was almost ready to take off and, determined not to miss his chance to join his bride, Raja headed straight for it. His security chief ran after him only to be waved away for so small a craft had only limited room for passengers.

Ruby buckled her belt in the small, stiflingly hot compartment. She had never flown in so small a plane before and she felt utterly unnerved by her solitary state. When a young man approached her with a bent head and a tray to proffer a glass she was quick to mutter grateful thanks and grasp it, drinking down the fragrantly scented chilled drink, only to wince at the bitter aftertaste it left in her mouth. She set the empty glass back on the tray with a strained smile and the steward retreated again.

A split second later, she heard someone else board and Raja dropped down into the seat by her side. Astonished by his reappearance, Ruby twisted round to study him. 'You've changed your mind? You're coming with me?'

Raja basked in the glowing smile of instant relief and appreciation she awarded him.

Ruby recalled him asking her if she was offering him a wedding night. Although she had said no, his change of heart made her worry that they had got their wires crossed. But wasn't that a stupid suspicion to cherish?

A guy with his looks would scarcely be so desperate that he would nurture such a desire for an unwilling woman.

The same young man reappeared with a second glass but when he focused on Raja, he suddenly froze and then he fell to his knees in the aisle and bowed his head very low, almost dropping the tray in the process.

Raja reached for the drink. The steward drew the tray back in apparent dismay and Raja had to lean out of his seat to grasp the glass.

'What's wrong with him?' Ruby whispered as the steward backed nervously out of the plane again. As the door slammed shut the engines began revving.

'He didn't realise who I was until he saw me up close. He must have assumed I was one of your guards when I boarded.'

The plane was turning. 'I have guards now?'

'I assume they're seated with the pilot. Of course you have guards,' Raja advanced, gulping back the drink and frowning at the acidic flavour. 'Wajid will have organised protection for you.'

As a wave of dizziness ran over Ruby she blinked and took a deep breath to clear her head. 'I'm feeling dizzy…it's probably nerves. I don't like small planes.'

'You'll be fine,' Raja reassured her.

Ruby's head was starting to feel too heavy for her neck and she propped her chin on the upturned palm of her hand.

'Are you feeling all right?' Raja asked as her head lowered.

'Just very, very tired,' she framed, her hands gripping the arms of her seat while the plane raced down the runway and rose into the air, the craft juddering while the engines roared.

'Not up to a wedding night?' Raja could not resist teasing her in an effort to take her mind off her nerves.

At that crack Ruby's head lifted and she turned to look at him. The plane was mercifully airborne.

The pupils of her eyes had shrunk to tiny pinpoints and Raja stared. 'Have you taken medication?' he asked her abruptly.

'No.' Ruby heard her voice slur. All of a sudden her tongue felt too big and clumsy for her mouth. 'Why?'

Raja could feel his own head reeling. 'There must have been something in that drink!' he exclaimed in disbelief, thrusting his hands down to rise out of the seat in one powerful movement.

'What…you…mean?' Ruby mumbled, her cheek sliding down onto her shoulder, her lashes drooping.

Raja staggered in the aisle and stretched out a hand to the door that led into the cockpit. But it was locked. Blinking rapidly, he shook his fuzzy head and hammered on the door, his arm dropping heavily down by his side again. Everything felt as if it were happening to him in slow motion. His legs crumpled beneath him and he fell on his knees, a bout of frustrated incredulous rage roaring up inside him and threatening to consume him. Ruby was slumped unconscious in her seat, her face hidden by her hair and he was in no state to protect her.

Ruby opened her eyes to darkness and strange sounds. Something was flapping and creaking and she could smell leather along with the faint aromatic hint of coffee. She was totally disorientated. Add in a pounding headache and the reality that her teeth were chattering with cold and she was absolutely miserable. She began slowly to shift her stiff, aching limbs and sit up. She was fully dressed but for her shoes and the ground was hard as a rock beneath her.

'What…where am I?' she mumbled thickly, the inside of her mouth as dry as a bone.

'Ruby?' It was Raja's deep accented drawl and she stiffened nervously at the awareness of movement and rustling in the darkness.

A match was struck and an oil lamp hanging on a tent pole cast illumination on the shadowy interior and the man towering over her. She blinked rapidly, relief engulfing her when she recognised Raja's powerful physique. Adjusting to the flickering light, her eyes clung to his hard bronzed features. In shocking defiance of the cold biting into her bones *he* was bare chested, well-defined hair-roughened pectorals flexing above the corrugated musculature of his abdomen. He was wearing only boxer shorts.

'My goodness, what happened to us?' Ruby demanded starkly, shivering violently as the chill of the air settled deeper into her clammy flesh. 'What are we doing in a tent?'

Raja crouched down on a level with her, long, strong thighs splayed. His stunning bone structure, composed of razor-sharp cheekbones, slashing angles and forbidding hollows, momentarily paralysed her and she simply stared, mesmerised by a glorious masculine perfection only enhanced by a dark haze of stubble.

'We were kidnapped and dumped out in the Ashuri desert. We have no phones, no way of communicating our whereabouts—'

'K-kidnapped?' Ruby stammered through rattling teeth. 'Why on earth would anyone want to kidnap us?'

'Someone who intended to prevent our marriage.'

'But we're *already*—'

'Married,' he slotted in flatly for her, handsome mouth hardening into a look of grim restraint as if being married was the worst thing that had ever happened to him but he was too polite to mention it. 'Obviously the kidnappers weren't aware of that when they planned this outrage. Apparently they assumed that our wedding would take place at the cathedral in Simis the day after tomorrow. In fact I believe a reconciliation and blessing service is actually planned for that afternoon.'

'Oh, my word,' she framed shakily, struggling to think clearly again. 'The kidnappers were trying to *stop* us from getting married? But if we're in the desert why is it so cold?'

'It *is* very cold here at night.' He swept up the quilt lying in a heap at her feet and wrapped it round her narrow shoulders.

'You're not cold,' she breathed almost resentfully, huddling into the folds of the quilt.

'No,' he acknowledged.

'Kidnapped,' she repeated shakily. 'That's not what I came out here for.'

'It may not be a comfort but I'm convinced that no

harm was intended to come to you. I was not supposed to be with you. I invited that risk by changing my travel plans at the eleventh hour and boarding the same flight,' the prince explained with sardonic cool. 'The kidnappers only wanted to prevent you from turning up for our wedding, a development which would have offended my people enough to bring protesters out into the streets.'

'So not everybody wants us to get married,' Ruby registered with a frown, shooting him an accusing glance. 'You didn't tell me that some people were so hostile to the idea of us marrying.'

'Common sense should have told you that but the objectors are in a minority in both countries.'

'How do you know all this?'

'Our captors were keen to explain their motives. The drugged drink didn't knock me out for as long as you. I began recovering consciousness as a pair of masked men were dragging us into this tent. Unfortunately I was so dizzy I could barely focus or stand and they pulled a gun on me. I don't think they had any intention of using it unless I managed to interfere with their escape,' he explained heavily and she could tell from his discomfited expression just how challenging he had found it to choose caution over courage. 'It would have been foolish to risk injury out here while you were incapacitated and without protection. I believe the men were mercenaries hired by a group of our subjects to ensure that you didn't turn up for the wedding—'

'*Our*...subjects?' she queried.

'We are in Ashur and the masked men were of Western origin...I think. Members of both royal households were aware of our travel plans so it will be hard to establish where the security leak occurred and who chose to take advantage of it and risk our lives. But it must be done—'

'At least we're not hurt.'

'That doesn't diminish the gravity of the crime.' Raja dealt her a stern appraisal. 'One of us could have had an allergic reaction to the drug we were given. Violence could have been used against us. Although our captors tried to talk as though this was intended to be a harmless prank, you might easily have suffered illness or injury alone out here. In addition, our disappearance will have cast both our countries into a very dangerous state of turmoil and panic.'

'Oh, hell,' Ruby groaned as he finished that sobering speech and she pushed her tousled hair off her brow and muttered in a small voice, 'My head hurts.'

He touched her hand, realised her fingers were cold as ice and concern indented his brow. 'I'll light a fire—there is enough wood.'

'What on earth are we going to do?'

With relaxed but economical movements, Raja began to light a small fire. 'A search for us will already have begun. The Najari air force will mount an efficient rescue mission but they have a very large area to cover. We have food and shelter. This is an oasis and *bedu* tribesmen must come here sometimes to water their flocks. Many of them have phones and could quickly summon help. I could trek out to find the nearest settlement but I am reluctant to leave you alone—'

'I would manage,' Ruby declared.

'I don't think so,' the prince told her without apology as a spark flared and he fed it with what appeared to be dried foliage. 'I will make tea.'

'I could come with you—'

'You couldn't stand the heat by day or keep up with me, which would put both of us at greater risk.'

Stymied by his conviction of her lack of stamina, Ruby dug her toes into the quilt in an effort to defrost them. 'How come you're so calm?'

'When all else fails, celebrate the positive and…we *are* safe and healthy.'

The warm drink did satisfy her thirst and drive off her inner chill though even the effort of sitting up to drink made her very aware of how tired and dizzy she still was.

'Try to get some sleep,' the prince advised.

The thin mat that was all that lay between her and the ground provided little padding. She curled up. Raja tucked the quilt round her as if she were a small child. The cold of the earth below pierced the mat, making her shiver again and, expelling his breath in an impatient hiss, Raja got below the quilt with her and melded his heated body to the back of hers.

'What are you doing?' Ruby squeaked, her slight figure stiff as a metal strut in the loose circle of his strong arms.

'There's no need for you to be cold while I am here.'

'You're not a hot-water bottle!' Ruby spat, unimpressed, her innate distrust of men rising like a shot of hot steam inside her.

'And you're not as irresistible as you seem to think,' Raja imparted silkily.

The heat of her angry suspicion blazed into mortification and if possible she became even more rigid. Ignoring the fact, Raja curled her back firmly into his amazingly warm body.

'I don't like this,' she admitted starchily.

'Neither do I,' Raja confided without skipping a beat. 'I'm more into sex than cuddling.'

Outrage glittered in her eyes in the flickering light from the dying fire. She wanted to thump him but the horrible cold was steadily receding from her body and she was afraid that she would look comically prudish if she fought physically free of his embrace.

'And just think,' Raja remarked lazily above her head. 'All those miserable old diehards who think we shouldn't be getting married will be so pleased to find out we *are* married now.'

'Why?'

'If you were still single your reputation would be ruined by spending the night out here alone with me. As it is you're a married woman and safe from the embarrassment of a scandal, if not much of a catch in the wife stakes.'

Ruby twisted her head around, brown eyes blazing. 'And what's that supposed to mean?'

'A sex ban would exude zero appeal for the average male in either one of our countries.'

'You signed up for it,' Ruby reminded him stubbornly, furious that he could be so basic that he deemed sex with a virtual stranger a necessary extra to a successful civilised relationship with a woman.

Raja was not thinking with intellect alone. In fact his brain had little to do with his reactions for he had a raging hard-on. Strands of fragrant silky blonde hair were brushing his shoulder, her pert derrière braced against his thighs while he had one hand resting just below the swell of a plump breast. He raised a knee to keep her out of contact with the seat of his arousal and tried to think of something, *anything* capable of cooling down the sexual fire in his blood.

## CHAPTER FIVE

WHEN Ruby wakened she was immediately conscious of the heat and the crumpled state of her clothing. What she wanted more than anything at that moment was access to a long, refreshing shower and opening her eyes on the interior of the roughly made and claustrophobic tent was not a heartening experience. She checked her watch and was taken aback to realise how long she had slept for it was already almost one in the afternoon.

Raja was nowhere to be seen and she sat up in a rush, pushing off the quilt and registering the presence of her suitcase in one corner. Mentally she leafed through what she recalled packing for what she had assumed would be short-term requirements while the majority of her wardrobe was shipped out in advance of her arrival. Just as Hermione had been shipped out, she recalled, her eyes suddenly stinging, for she missed her dog and knew her quirky little pet would be sadly missing her. She scrambled up and looked in vain for her shoes before peering out of the tent in search of Raja. It was not that she needed him, it was just she wanted to know where he was, she told herself staunchly.

That angle forgotten, however, Ruby remained standing stock still to stare out of the tent with a dropped jaw at the view of an alien world that shook her to the core. As far as the eye could see there was nothing but sand and the occasional small bush on a wide flat plain overarched by a bright blue sky and baked by a sun so bright and hot she couldn't look directly at it.

'Coffee? You slept soundly,' Raja commented from the side of the small fire he had lit below the ample tent canopy.

'Like the proverbial log.' One glance in his direction and Ruby's teeth grated together in exasperation. As if it weren't hot as hell already he had to build a fire to sit beside! And there he sat, infuriatingly immaculate in the same long off-white robe he had donned the day before and seemingly as comfortable living in the desert as he might have been in a five-star hotel. Only the reality that he was unshaven marked his departure from his usual standards of perfect grooming.

'Where did you get more water to make coffee?' Ruby was struggling not to care that her hair was probably standing on end and mascara had to be smeared all round her eyes.

'This is an oasis. I established that last night. An underground stream feeds a pool below the cliff and our water supply is secure.' He gestured to the other side of the tent. 'Do you want a drink?'

Ruby flipped round to belatedly note the towering cliff of rock on the far side of the tent. A large grove of flourishing date palms and other vegetation made it clear that a water source had to exist somewhere near by. 'I'd sooner not take the risk. After what happened on the plane, I'm only drinking water that comes out of a bottle,' she told him thinly.

The prince compressed his sensual mouth on the laugh he almost let escape. She looked very small, young and unsure of herself, standing there with tousled hair and bare feet, clearly unsettled by her surroundings but struggling not to reveal the fact. She hated to betray weakness and it was a trait he implicitly understood. Dishevelled though she was, however, her hair still glinted like polished silk and her flawless skin had the subdued glow of a pearl. Her beauty was not dependent on cosmetics or the flattering cut and gloss of designer clothing, he recognised, very much impressed by how good she looked without those trimmings. 'There is no bottled water to be had here.'

'Yes, I know that…I'm not stupid!' Ruby snapped back at him in furious self-defence. 'I just don't do the camping thing…OK? Never did do it, never saw the appeal of it and don't want to be roughing it out here now!'

'That is very understandable,' the prince responded with the utmost cool.

Far from impervious to the likely impression she had to be making on a guy who had probably majored in advanced desert survival skills during the war, Ruby dealt him a dirty look. 'I don't care if you laugh at me!'

Retreating crossly back into the tent because she cared very much indeed, Ruby hauled her case to the ground and opened it. She was grateful she hadn't bothered to lock it because, like her shoes, her handbag in which she would have stowed a key was missing. Only when she saw the state of the tumbled contents did she realise how naive she was being: their kidnappers had clearly rummaged through the contents before unloading it from the plane, doubtless keen to ensure that she hadn't packed a phone. She dug out her wash bag and a towel as well as a change of clothing and a pair of sneakers, suddenly very grateful indeed to be in possession of such necessities. A quick inspection of the tent interior warned her that Raja had not been so fortunate.

Donning fresh underwear and tee, she wrapped a sarong round her waist and tried to move more slowly because the heat was making her perspire. She came to a reluctant halt on the edge of the sparse shade offered by the canopy. 'I have a new toothbrush and a razor you can have and you can share my towel.'

In the mood his wife was in, Raja considered that a surprisingly generous offer. A wolfish grin of appreciation slashed his bold, bronzed features and he looked so ravishingly handsome at that instant that Ruby stared fixedly at him, her tummy flipping like an acrobat on a high wire, the warmth of awareness sending hot colour surging into her oval face.

She climbed up the slope and saw the pool that had formed in a gully densely shaded by the massive bulk of the rock formation behind it. Raja strode up from the tent to join her and fell into step beside her, his hand first at her elbow and then at her spine to help her ascend the rougher ground and to steady her when she wavered. He had incredibly good manners and, unused as she was to that consideration from a man, she could only be pleased that he was willing to make the effort. She was uneasily aware that so far she had not been the most heartening companion. Even worse in so challenging and harsh an environment she could only be at a loss.

They hovered by the side of the palm-fringed, crystal-clear pool formed by the water seeping out from a crack low in the rock face. Ruby moved first, taking off her sneakers to dip her toes in the water. The temperature was deliciously cool on her skin in the intense heat. Lifting her chin and refusing to be self-conscious, she wasted no time in pulling her tee shirt off and untying the sarong. In bra and knickers she reckoned that she was as well covered as she would have been in a bikini. Raja followed suit, stripping off his long tunic and draping it over a rock beside her clothing. Wide-eyed, Ruby watched the sleek muscles working in his strong back and shoulders and then hurriedly averted her gaze, reminding herself how much she had always hated her stepfather leering at her body. It was a clumsy comparison though, she reflected, for she suspected that Raja might well enjoy her admiration.

Standing thigh deep in the pool, Raja watched Ruby wash, his masculine body quickening with hungrily appreciative male interest. Wet through, her underwear was very revealing. He could see the prominent pink nipples poking through the sheer cups of her bra and he wondered how sensitive she would be if he put his mouth to those delicate peaks. As she waded out of the pool again, the clinging fabric of her panties clearly outlined the cleft between her thighs and the forbidden aspect of what he was seeing was a much more stimulating sight than complete nudity. Hard as steel in response, he studied the rippling surface of the water instead. On a very basic level his thoughts were reminding him that she was his wife, that at the very least he was entitled to look while at the same time his brain was recalling their agreement. No sex, no touching. Why the hell had he ever agreed to that? He reckoned that if he touched her the way he was feeling the force of his desire would frighten her.

Ruby walked out of the water and reached for the towel to dab herself dry, moving out of the shade in the expectation that the sun would dry her off more quickly.

'This is the hottest hour of the day. Cover up or you'll burn,' Raja warned her, knowing that he was burning already in an altogether more primitive way.

Reckoning that he was bone-deep bossy in the same unalterable way that holly leaves were prickly, Ruby ignored the stricture and left off her tee. She knotted the sarong just above her bra and began to comb out her damp hair, her attention quite naturally straying to his sleek powerful physique as he stood in the water that had covered her to the waist. His torso was a streamlined wall of muscle, his bulging upper arms, narrow hips and long thighs whipcord taut with lean tensile strength. As he splashed water up over his magnificent body, droplets glistening like diamonds in the bright light, she noticed the revealing fit of his boxer shorts which clearly defined his manhood. Feeling like a voyeur invading his privacy, she quickly looked away but she was shocked.

Was the presence of her only minimally clad body responsible for putting him in that condition? Her face stung with mortified red at the suspicion. What else was she supposed to think? She might not be irresistible as he had quipped the night before but she evidently did have what it took to awaken the most basic chemistry of all. It also occurred to her that she really had not realised until now that an aroused male would be quite so...*large* in that department.

A heavy ache stirred low within her own body and she was taken aback by the recognition that seeing Raja aroused, and knowing that her body was responsible for that development, excited her. And it was the first time ever that a man had had that astounding effect on Ruby. Indeed as a rule she felt uneasy and apprehensive when boyfriends became too enthusiastic in her arms. But then Ruby had never been comfortable with either her body or her own sexuality. How could she have been? During the years that had seen her steadily transform from child to young woman she had been forced to live with her stepfather's obscene comments and the lecherous looks he had constantly aimed at her developing body. While being careful to ensure that her mother neither heard nor saw anything amiss, Curtis Sommerton had taught his stepdaughter to be ashamed of her femininity. His barely concealed lust had made Ruby feel soiled. Although he had never managed to unleash that lust on her, he had taught her an aversion to the male body and the kind of crude sexist comments that some men found amusing.

The prince draped the damp towel carefully round

Ruby's bare shoulders. 'Your skin is very fair. Sit in the shadows while I finish here.'

And because Ruby was getting too hot under the sun and her confusing thoughts preoccupied her she did as she was told in most un-Ruby-like silence. She watched him peer into the tiny compact mirror she had produced for his use and shave and then clean those perfect, even white teeth. Her curiosity about him on a personal level was leapfrogging up the scale at an embarrassing rate. Had she had access to the Internet she would have been searching out information about his social life. He *had* to have one. As much of a pin-up as a movie star, rich as sin and obviously possessed of a healthy male libido, Raja al-Somari had to have women in his life. Did he enjoy discreet affairs? He would have to be discreet because Najar was a conservative country just like Ashur. Did he seek out lovers only when he was abroad? Or did he have a lover stashed away somewhere more convenient? The intimate aspect of her thoughts mortified her. What was it to her, for goodness' sake? Even if he had a constant procession of women eager to provide him with an outlet for his sexual needs, it was none of her business!

Having replaced the long tunic, his black hair curling back damply from his brow, Raja approached her. 'We should eat now.'

He showed her the ancient refrigerator operating off a car battery in the back of the tent.

'You understand this way of life,' Ruby remarked.

'When I was a child my father often sent me to stay with my uncle in the desert. He is the ruling sheikh of a nomadic tribe,' he explained. 'But in Najar there are few true nomads left now. The *bedu* have settled so that their children can attend school and they have easier access to jobs and medical facilities. But the nomadic way of life is still quite popular in Ashur.'

There was only fruit, some vegetables, meat and bread in the refrigerator and several tins of indistinguishable supplies. 'I assume we're not expected to be here for very long,' Raja commented, handing her a cup of coffee.

Ruby frowned up at what looked like a red flag rippling on top of the cliff. 'What's that up there?'

'A blanket I tied to a stick. It will be easily visible from the air and unusual enough to attract attention—'

'You *climbed* up there?' Ruby exclaimed, aghast, for the cliff rose to a pinnacle of almost vertical rock.

'It was not so difficult.' Raja shrugged a broad shoulder that dismissed the risk involved in so dangerous a climb. 'I went up to take advantage of the view and see if there was any sign of human habitation but there is nothing within sight.'

'Obviously this particular place was chosen because it was isolated,' Ruby said wryly. 'At least I don't have any family to worry about me—what about you?'

'A father, a younger brother and two sisters and a whole host of other relatives. But I'm most worried about my father. He is not strong. The stress my disappearance will cause will endanger his health,' he proffered, his wide sensual mouth compressing, his handsome features taut with concern. 'But there is nothing I can do about it.'

Her generous heart was troubled by his apprehension. 'I have no relatives in Ashur, have I?'

'None close that I'm aware of. Distant cousins, certainly.'

His ability to efficiently feed them both set Ruby's teeth on edge. He could cook on an open fire with very limited ingredients and produce an edible meal while she would have been challenged to do so even in a modern kitchen. Her mother had been a poor cook and Ruby's own repertoire was limited to the making or heating of simple snacks. While she lived with Stella, a very competent cook, her lack in that field had not seemed important but somehow in Raja's presence it annoyed the hell out of her.

Feeling helpless stung Ruby's strong pride. She hated feeling reliant on Raja and was painfully conscious that to date she had proved more of a burden than a help. That sense of inadequacy drove her into ceaseless activity that afternoon. She tidied up her clothes, ashamed of the fact she had left the garments lying in a tumbled heap beside her suitcase. She folded the quilts, shook the sand off the mats and took care of the few dishes and then she wandered round the grove of date palms busily gathering twigs and dried foliage to keep the fire going. The heat sapped her energy fast and she was filled with dismay at the prospect of what the much higher summer temperatures had to be like to live with. Her hair sticking to the back of her neck, she headed up to the pool to cool off again. The cold water felt glorious. Wrapped in the sarong, she sat down wearily on a rock in the deep shade to knot her hair and hold it off her perspiring face, wishing she had something to tie it back with. She looked across the pool to see her desert prince approaching, all six feet plus of his leanly muscled commanding figure pure poetry in motion, and she pursed her lips.

There he was drop-dead gorgeous and rich and he could cook, as well. She marvelled that he had stayed single so long. Of course that authoritarian streak might be a problem for some. He knew best…*always*. Her shoulders were pink and slightly burned as he had warned before lunch and she wasn't one bit grateful that his forecast had come true but she knew that she ought to be grateful that he was so well able to cope when she was not. He was also equally keen to protect her from her own mistakes.

'Watch out for—'

Ruby lifted her hands in a sudden silencing motion, brown eyes lightening with temper. 'Just let it go, Raja. I'll take my chances against whatever it is! You're just about perfect and you know everything and you could probably live out here all year but I'm afraid I'm not cut from the same cloth.'

'The desert is home to my people and yours,' the prince contradicted in a tone of reproof. 'We design and maintain beautiful gardens and parks in Najar but when our people want to get back to basics they come out into the desert.'

Ruby snatched in a sustaining breath and she kicked a rock with a sneaker-clad foot to expel her extreme irritation.

'Ruby!'

As the rock rolled over and something moved and darted from beneath it Raja almost leapt forward in his haste to haul her out of harm's way. From several feet away, plastered back against the solid support of his hard muscular frame, Ruby stared in horror at the greenish yellow insects rushing out.

'Scorpions. They shelter in dark places during the day. Their sting is very painful,' Raja informed her as she went limp against him, sick with repulsion at how close she had come to injury. He removed her to a safe distance.

'I don't like insects either,' Ruby confided in a shaken rush. 'Especially ones that size and anything that stings—'

'There are also poisonous snakes—'

'Shut up...*shut up*!' she launched at him fiercely. 'I'm not on an educational trip. I don't want to know!'

Raja turned her round and stared down at her, eyes shimmering with reluctant amusement.

'I don't care what you say either,' Ruby added truculently. 'Give it a rest—stop trying to train me into being a stuffy royal who never puts a foot wrong!'

This time Raja al-Somari laughed out loud, his ready sense of humour finally breaking free of his innate reserve, for Ruby was very much an original and not at all like the women he was accustomed to meeting. She didn't flirt—at least if she did, she didn't bother to do it with him. Indeed she used no feminine wiles that he could identify. She staged no enticing poses to draw attention to her body. She made no attempt to appeal to his ego with compliments or to pay him any especially gratifying attention and she had not told him a single story calculated to present her in a flattering light. He had never in his entire life met a woman as uncomplicated as she was and the more he was exposed to her frank, fearless style, the more he liked it.

'So, you do have a sense of humour after all. My goodness, is that a relief!' Ruby exclaimed, shaking her head in emphasis, a wealth of damp strands escaping her loose knot and spilling across her shoulders.

Raja stared down at her stunning face and the teasing smile on her ripe rosy lips. He lowered his handsome, dark head almost jerkily as if he were being yanked down to her level by some mysterious but very powerful outside force. He found her soft, sultry mouth with his and although that kiss started out gentle and searching it heated up at supersonic speed. Desire rose to gush through Ruby in a floodtide. Nothing had ever felt so necessary as the hard pressure of that sensual mouth on hers and the taste of him drowned her senses like a shot of alcohol on a weak head.

Without a word, Raja released her with startling abruptness and pressed a hand to her spine to urge her back down the slope towards the tent.

Ruby had never experienced such a charge of hunger before and, suddenly deprived of that connection with him, she was in a daze. The tip of her tongue snaked out to explore the reddened and swollen contours of her lips and all she could think about was how much she wanted his hot, hungry mouth back on hers again. The strength of that craving shook her. Her nipples were tight and tingling and her legs felt shaky. Putting one foot in front of another was a challenge. And at the same time, gallingly she was desperate to know what he was thinking.

Outside the tent Ruby shot Raja a sidewise glance brimming with curiosity. His hard profile was taut and he skimmed a look back at her, eyes brilliant with a wealth of stormy emotion. That shook her and in response her heart started beating very, very fast. 'Don't play games with me, Ruby,' he spelled out in a roughened undertone.

Games? Ruby was offended by the suggestion and she lifted her chin in denial. 'I don't know what you're talking about—*you* kissed *me*—'

'But you made no objection. When you have said that you don't want me to touch you what else is that but a game?'

'I don't calculate things to that extent. You are so suspicious,' Ruby condemned, flushed and flustered by the reminder and by the embarrassment of her own uncharacteristic behaviour. 'It's being in this situation…I simply forgot and got carried away for a moment.'

'Every action has consequences,' Raja pronounced, rigid with the pent-up force of arousal he was restraining, his lean hands clenching into fists, for his body was not one half as disciplined as his quick and clever brain.

Ruby sank down on a mat inside the tent. It was hot but nothing was as hot and disturbing as the hum of unnatural warmth at the centre of her body, which was shockingly new and demanding. She could not relax. She lifted a hand, watched it tremble and tried and failed to laugh at the state she was in. One kiss and it had been earth-shattering, even more so than the last. Now she felt cheated. She wanted more, she wanted to know what it felt like to make love with a man who attracted her to that extent. The hurricane-force potency of that attraction was certainly a first. She had not experienced anything comparable with other men when intimacy had often felt like more of a threat and a nuisance than a potential source of pleasure. More than once her unenthusiastic response had led to her being asked if she was frigid or gay. She had often had to fight her way out of over-keen encounters. She had had to shout, she had had to defend and justify her boundaries because the easy availability of sex was often taken for granted in relationships. But not once, not once in the five years since she began dating had she actually *wanted* to make love.

And now what was she doing about it? Here she was taking refuge in the tent and avoiding Raja as if she were ashamed of herself or afraid when she was neither, she conceded uncertainly. It was not as though she could fall pregnant either, she reminded herself squarely. Some months earlier her doctor had advised her to agree to a course of contraceptive pills in the hope of correcting an irregular menstrual cycle. Although she had no supply with her in the desert she assumed she would still be protected for some time against conception. She lifted her head high. She had not been playing some sexual game with Raja, she was not a tease and didn't want him thinking that she was. In an impatient movement she scrambled upright again.

Raja was staring into the dying embers of the fire, black lashes lowered and as spectacular even in profile as glossy black fringes, his high cheekbones prominent, sculptured mouth clenched.

'I wasn't playing games,' Ruby declared defiantly.

He flung his proud dark head back and looked straight at her. 'I want you so much I ache…'

And his admission sizzled through Ruby like a hot knife gliding through butter. His confidence shocked her, for she had believed that she was being bold but his words made hers meaningless and little more than a sulky expression of innocence. Indeed almost a lie, she adjusted uncomfortably, jolted by her sudden unexpected collision with the scorching challenge of his gaze. Just at that moment she knew that she had sought him out again quite deliberately and that he was experienced enough to know it.

'A woman hasn't made me ache since I was younger than you are now,' Raja told her huskily, vaulting upright with an easy grace of movement that tensed every muscle in her slim body. 'You're very beautiful…'

So was he, but she was too wary and proud to tell him that that lean dark-angel beauty of his had taken up residence in her brain and dug talon claws of need and desire into her very soul. When he kissed her she felt as dizzy and uncoordinated as though she had drunk too much alcohol. He made her feel out of control and she didn't like that but, regardless of that fact, every time she looked at him it was a tougher challenge to look away again. She moved closer and somehow he met her in the middle, a possessive hand closing on her slight shoulder to hold her in place, his mouth or was it her mouth eagerly melding with the temptation of his again. And that crushing kiss was good, *so* good, her bare toes curled and her nerve endings sang. Her arms went round him, her fingers spearing into his hair, and with her eager encouragement his mouth got rougher and harder, his lean, powerful length sealing more forcefully to her softer curves.

It was too much: she couldn't breathe, broke her mouth free to pant for breath and yet immediately sought him out again with renewed hunger and blindly impatient hands. In the midst of it he eased back from her to haul off his robe but just as quickly he pulled her back into his arms. The sarong fell at her feet but she didn't notice because Raja was already lowering her down on the quilts while pressing taut open-mouthed kisses along the slender expanse of her neck. She squirmed helplessly as the tip of his tongue scored the pulse there and then he nipped at her responsive flesh with his strong white teeth. Need was driving her now, all the while the heat in her pelvis was building and building into a furnace.

Her bra fell away. His palm closed over a small, pert breast and she gasped, back arching as he plunged his mouth down to the swollen pink tip and let his teeth graze the straining nipple. She dragged him up to kiss him again and ran an appreciative palm down over the hair-roughened expanse of his superb torso. He caught her hand in his and brought her fingers down to the rampant length of the shaft straining against his hard flat stomach. A shudder ran through his big frame as she took that invitation and stroked him, moulding the smooth hard heat and promise of him with reverent fingers.

He moved her beneath him and again put his carnal mouth to her tender nipples. He was gentle at first but still she writhed and when he got a little more ardent she cried out, struggling to find herself again in the thunderous, greedy surge of the hunger he had awakened.

'Very beautiful,' Raja groaned in reply. 'And wonderfully passionate...'

The hollow ache between her thighs had her hips shifting back and forth. He traced the tender pink flesh there and she shivered, violently and with longing, driven by feverish want and need. He slid a finger into her and she was hot and wet and tight and he groaned with masculine appreciation, capturing her lips with his again, letting his tongue dart into the sensitive interior of her mouth with a skilful flick that made the blood drum insanely fast through her veins.

He teased the tiny bundle of nerve endings that controlled her entire body and she writhed in the storm of intoxicating sensation. 'Don't stop...whatever you do, don't stop!' she warned him through gritted teeth, reacting to an overload of pleasure that wiped out every thought and consideration and left frantic desire in charge.

Black hair tousled, golden eyes hot as flames, the prince rose over her. 'After this, there is no going back.'

In the merciless grip of unsated need, Ruby could barely focus on his darkly handsome features. 'No going back?' she repeated blankly.

Raja, as eager for completion as she was, was already pressing back her thighs and impatiently splaying his hands below her hips to raise her to him. As he positioned himself and pushed into her a sharp pain arrowed through her and she cried out. He stopped moving to gaze down at her with a bemused frown. 'What's wrong?'

'Nothing...don't stop,' Ruby told him, taut with discomfiture for it had not occurred to her that losing her virginity might hurt. Her more experienced friend, Stella, might have told her a lot of things but that possibility had not been mentioned.

Dark eyes confused, he stared down at her. 'But I hurt you.'

Ruby could feel her face getting hotter and hotter. 'It's my first time...that's all. No big deal.'

It was Raja's turn to be surprised and it was a very big deal on his terms. His bride was a virgin? The level of his ignorance about her annoyed him. He had made the wrong assumptions but not without her encouragement to do so. A slight shudder racked him as he endeavoured to remain still while every fibre of his being craved the completion of sinking into her as far and as fast as he could go.

'It's all right...it really is,' Ruby whispered, deeply embarrassed by the enforced pause in their lovemaking.

The prince lowered his head and pressed a kiss to the rosy invitation of her mouth. For the very first time he allowed himself to think of her as his wife. It was a powerful source of attachment for a man given to ruthlessly guarding his emotions. Lithe as a cat, he shifted inside her and her eyes widened with wondering appreciation as the first swirl of sensation circled her pelvis and melted her inside to hot, liquid honey.

*'Oh...'* she framed, taken aback by that feeling of exquisite fullness, lips parting, eyes drifting shut on a heady vocal sound of appreciation.

'I want it to be good for you…'

Ruby looked up at him, her entire body buzzing with electrified arousal. 'It's better than good…'

Raja shifted again, initially slow and sure, patiently teaching her his rhythm while he revelled in the velvety grip of her slick passage. In the still heat of the tent, perspiration gleaming on his sleek bronzed length, he pleasured her with long driving strokes. Excitement gripped her as the pace quickened and the only thing that mattered then was the pounding surge of his body into hers. Delirious with the pulsing pleasure, she arched her back and wild tremors tore through her. With a feverish cry she splintered into the electrifying heat of an earth-shattering climax.

Afterwards, Raja held her close, soothing fingers caressing the smooth skin of her abdomen while little quivers, aftershocks of that intense physical crescendo, still coursed through her. 'I'm sorry I hurt you. If I had known that you were not experienced I would have been more gentle.'

Hugging a glorious unfamiliar sense of well-being along with the feeling that she was still floating on a fluffy cloud, Ruby fixed dazed eyes on his face. 'I'm not sure gentle would have been quite so exciting.'

Raja laughed with easy appreciation and vaulted upright. He pulled on his boxers and strode out of the tent. She wondered what he was doing but was too lazy to ask or follow as she lay there with limbs that felt weighted down. At the corner of her mind a kernel of unease was nagging at her, keen to remind her that she had trashed the platonic agreement she had forged with Raja and made their relationship much more personal, much more intimate than she had ever envisaged.

Just at that moment such serious reflections seemed ridiculously irrelevant. They were marooned in the desert in circumstances neither of them could ever have foreseen and, as far as she was concerned, the normal rules no longer applied. It was just sex, she told herself urgently, not worth getting worked up about. Creating a fuss about it would only make her look deeply uncool.

Raja strode back in and knelt down by her side. One glimpse of that strong, dark face and sleek physique and her tummy flipped and her brain seemed to turn to mush. He smiled down at her, and it was, without a doubt, the most spectacular smile. Evidently her approval rating had gone from zero to through the roof. He reached down to uncurl her legs for she was lying coiled in a ball.

'What are you doing?' she muttered in bewilderment.

He didn't answer, he simply showed her. He had soaked the towel in the pool and wrung it out. Beneath her stunned gaze he began to run that very welcome cold, wet cloth over her hot, damp body, cooling her feverish temperature, leaving her fresh and revitalised and unexpectedly touched by his thoughtfulness.

They ate in a surprisingly comfortable silence below the tent canopy. 'I don't think we'll be here for much longer,' Raja admitted quietly. 'Once the fact that we were married in the UK is publicly announced there can be no reason for leaving us here.'

'But that means that someone would have to own up to knowing where we are.'

'There are many ways of passing information without the source being identified,' the man by her side remarked shrewdly.

When she finished her drink and began to get up he rose with her and pulled her up against his powerful frame. Hot eyes raked her flushed and uncertain face and for an instant she was stiff, suddenly disturbingly lost in the brave new world of intimacy she had created with him. The balance of power had changed irrevocably. A low-pitched growl vibrating in his throat, Raja closed a hand into her tumbled hair and kissed her, hard and hungrily, unleashing a passion that was uninhibited. He thrust aside the sarong and cupped her bare breasts, teasing the tips between thumb and finger. An arrowing tingle of damp heat speared between her thighs and she ached. She quivered and clung, wanting and needing again even more than she had the first time.

# CHAPTER SIX

RUBY suffered a rude awakening the next morning. Raja was shaking her shoulder, the tent walls were flapping loudly and her ears were ringing with noise.

'Get dressed,' he framed urgently as she blinked in bewilderment. 'We've been found and we're leaving!'

As he strode from the tent she peered out after him and saw a pair of what looked like heavy-duty military helicopters coming in to land. Galvanised into action as she registered that their desert sojourn appeared to be at an end, she yanked open her case in search of something decent to wear. She dressed in haste, choosing cropped trousers and a vest top teamed with a light shirt. As she hastily brushed her hair every movement she made ensured that she remained mortifyingly conscious of the intimate ache between her legs.

The events of the past twelve hours raced through her memory and her slender hands fisted in defensive rejection of her reckless behaviour. As a rule, Ruby didn't *do* reckless. Ruby was usually thoughtful and cautious, never impulsive, yet she had, with very little thought, utterly destroyed the platonic marital agreement she had insisted on. All for what? Great sex, she acknowledged shamefacedly, but in the aftermath even greater regrets.

They had agreed to a fake marriage and now how was their relationship to be defined? The agreement had been broken, the boundaries blurred and their respective roles were no longer clear-cut. Raja's unqualified passion had enthralled her. She had to be honest with herself about that. She found the Najari prince regent incredibly attractive. He fascinated her and he had tempted her from that first kiss back in England. No other man had ever had that effect on her. She had been eager to know what sex was all about, had wanted to feel what other women felt and had sensed from the outset that he might well be the guy who could show her. And he had, unquestionably, shown her. Over and over and over again, she recalled, her face burning. In bed her desert prince ditched all reserve and cool in favour of a scorching-hot sexual intensity that had lit a fire inside her that she could neither resist nor quench.

As Ruby emerged from the tent she saw Raja standing in conversation with several men, all of whom wore military uniform. Every male eye turned towards her and then heads inclined and lowered and a respectful murmur of greeting acknowledged her presence. Raja drew her forward with an assured hand to introduce her to the various air-force personnel before assisting her into the nearest helicopter.

'We will breakfast in Najar—'

'I think I should stay in Ashur for the moment,' Ruby told him quietly. 'I ought to continue on to where I was heading when we were kidnapped.'

The tall black-haired male by her side frowned down at her.

'Naturally you want to let your father see that you're OK as soon as possible. I'll be fine,' she asserted lightly.

Raja captured her hand in his. 'Where's your wedding ring?'

Ruby glanced down at her bare fingers. 'Oh, dear, I didn't notice. It was very loose and it must've fallen off. I don't think it was still on my finger when we arrived here.'

His wide sensual mouth compressed. 'I will find a replacement.'

A slight hint of amusement on her gaze, Ruby sent him an airy glance as though the matter was too trivial to discuss. 'No hurry…'

His face hardened, inky lashes dropping low over his intent scrutiny. 'We must agree to disagree,' he traded huskily. 'I will see you tonight—'

*'Tonight?'* Ruby was surprised, having assumed that their separation would last somewhat longer. She was also rather keen to have a decent breathing space in which to regroup.

'Tonight,' Raja confirmed, striding off to speak to the pilot before climbing aboard the second helicopter.

During the flight, when Ruby felt nervous tension beginning to rise at the prospect of what expectations might await her in Simis, the capital of Ashur, she breathed in deep. She reminded herself that she was reasonably intelligent, even-tempered and willing to learn, not to mention being filled with good intentions.

She didn't need Raja by her side telling her what to do every minute of the day.

The airport building outside Simis was a large temporary shed. Surrounded by soldiers and police who made her nervous, Ruby was greeted by Wajid Sulieman's familiar and surprisingly welcome face and tucked straight into a waiting car. His concerned questions about her health and how she had managed in the desert brought a smile to her expressive mouth.

'I was lucky to have the prince with me,' she admitted, willing to award honour where it was due. 'How did you find us?'

'Someone contacted the media with your location,' Wajid told her. 'From the moment that we announced that you were missing, people began gathering outside the palace gates to wait for news. There was great anger and concern on your behalf. Some were quick to suspect the Najaris of duplicity and there were protests. It was a very tense situation.'

'I'm sure feelings ran equally high in Najar,' Ruby remarked as the car cut around a horse and cart.

'Even higher. Your husband is a war hero and tremendously popular,' Wajid said. 'It is unfortunate that he was unable to accompany you here but I understand that he will be arriving later.'

'Yes.' Crowds lined the old-fashioned city streets and necks were craned to get a better view of her car. 'Are those people actually waiting to see me?' Ruby whispered incredulously.

'There is great excitement and curiosity about your arrival. It is a positive event after so many years of bad news,' the older man volunteered wryly. 'For the next few days you will be out and about a good deal to allow people to become familiar with you. The photograph taken after your wedding was very well received. I cannot praise Prince Raja highly enough for having had the foresight to organise it.'

'Raja thinks of everything,' Ruby agreed, thinking sunburn, scorpions…sex. A little tremor of heated recollection rippled low in her body and she stiffened, annoyed that even memory could make her so sensually susceptible.

On her short visit to Ashur as a teenager she had seen the imposing grey building that comprised the palace only from the vantage point of the tall wrought-iron gates. A step in the imperious wake of Wajid, she entered the palace from a side entrance where a group of staff bowed low and several introductions were offered. From the hall she was escorted up a staircase.

'Your uncle, the late King Tamim and his family used the east wing. I thought you might be more comfortable in this more modern corner of the palace.'

Ruby reckoned that only in Wajid's parlance could a décor at least sixty years out of date be deemed modern. 'What was my uncle like?'

'He was rather set in his ways, as was his daughter, Princess Bariah—'

'My cousin.'

'A fine young woman, who was of course destined to marry Prince Raja before the accident that took her life and that of her parents,' the older man remarked in his pedantic manner, quite unaware of Ruby coming to a sudden halt and shooting him a look of dismay.

Her cousin had originally been contracted to marry Raja? Of course that made sense but it was still the first time that that fact had been mentioned to Ruby. And like a bolt from the blue that little fact cut Ruby to the bone. Just at that moment it was a deeply unwelcome reminder that there was nothing personal, private or indeed special about her relationship with the future king of Najar and Ashur, for Raja had been equally willing, it seemed, to marry her cousin. Fate had simply served Ruby up in her cousin's stead. But how had Raja really felt about that sudden exchange of brides? Had he been attached to her royal cousin, Princess Bariah? A sliver like a shard of ice sliced through Ruby, who was affronted and hurt by the idea that she might well have been a second-best choice on her husband's terms. No doubt he would have been equally willing to share a bed with her cousin. How could she have been foolish enough to allow such intimacy without good reason? And how could desire alone ever be sufficient justification?

As she stepped through a door a little dog barked wildly and hurled itself at her legs. Smiling happily, Ruby got down on her knees to pet Hermione, who gave her a frantic squirming welcome before finally snuggling into her owner's arms and tucking her little head blissfully below Ruby's chin. Wajid mentioned the reconciliation service to be held at the cathedral that afternoon, which Ruby had to attend, as well as an evening reception at which she was to meet many important people. She stifled a groan at the thought of her inadequate wardrobe and wondered if the red suit could be freshened up for the occasion.

A knock sounded on the door and a young woman joined them. 'This is Zuhrah, Your Royal Highness, who with the assistance of your personal staff will take care of all your needs,' Wajid explained. 'She speaks excellent English.'

Zuhrah explained that she would look after Ruby's diary and take care of all the invitations she received. Wajid departed while the pretty brunette showed Ruby through the spacious suite of rooms that had been set aside for her use. Over the light lunch that was served in the dining area Ruby mentioned the red suit and Zuhrah wasted no time in going off to track it down. As soon as she had eaten Ruby took advantage of the bathroom—she would never take one for granted again—and enjoyed a long, invigorating shower. Having dried her hair, she returned to the drawing room, clad in a wrap, and asked Zuhrah, who was tapping out notes on a netbook, if her missing handbag had turned up. Apparently it had not and Ruby knew she would have to see a doctor if she wanted another contraceptive pill. But did she need to take that precaution now? Was she planning to continue sleeping with Raja?

She thought not. Her brain said no, a very firm no. A mistake was a mistake and better acknowledged as such. There was another consequence to be feared as well, she reminded herself ruefully. She had missed taking her contraceptive pills while she was in the desert and there had to be a risk that she might already have conceived a child by Raja. What was she going to do if that happened? A chill ran down Ruby's spine at the prospect of such a dilemma. She loved babies but a baby that would be deemed royal would severely complicate her practical marriage and ultimately wreck any hope of them establishing a civilised relationship. She was convinced that if she had a child there was no way that Raja would agree to her taking that child back home to the UK with her again.

The service at the cathedral late that afternoon required nothing more from Ruby than her presence. Police stood outside the historic building with linked arms to hold back the crowds struggling to catch a glimpse of the new princess. The evening reception was a great deal more taxing, however, for while she was perfectly able to make small talk she was embarrassed several times by more probing questions concerning her background than she wished to answer. People were extremely curious about her and as yet she did not have the skill to deflect unwelcome queries. Later she would register that she had known the exact moment when Raja entered the big reception room for a flutter of excitement seemed to run through the gathered cliques. With a muttered apology, Wajid left her side and heads turned away from her, eyes swerving towards the door while a low buzz of comment sounded.

'*Real* royalty,' someone whispered appreciatively within Ruby's hearing. 'And you can definitely tell the difference.'

Mortified heat burnished Ruby's fair complexion. *Real* royalty? Had she performed her role so badly? But then she knew that she could only be a pretend princess by virtue of her birth. How could she be anything else when she had spent all her life to date living as an ordinary person? But she was *trying*, she was trying very hard to be polite, reserved and dignified as Wajid had advised her she must be at all times while carefully avoiding controversial subjects. It was tough advice for a bubbly and naturally outspoken young woman to follow. To Ruby it also felt like trying to be something she was not while putting on airs and graces that went against the grain.

His tall powerful physique sheathed in a dove-grey suit, her husband looked devastatingly handsome. Her *husband*? Why was she thinking of Raja in such terms? He wasn't her husband, not really, she told herself angrily, irritated by the mental mistake. A woman chose her husband with her heart but she had not. Guilty colour mantling her face, Ruby studied that lean, strong, wondrously handsome face and she steeled herself to feel nothing, absolutely nothing. She watched Raja work the room like a professional, smooth and practised and yet charming as well with a word here, a greeting there, for some a smile, for others a more serious aspect. He was a class act socially, everything she was not. Hovering at his elbow, Wajid Sulieman looked as though all his Christmases had come at once.

When refreshments were served, Raja was finally free to join Ruby. Lustrous dark eyes gleaming like polished amber flared down into hers while he rested a light hand at her spine. She went rigid, rejecting the temptation of even that much familiarity while recalling Bariah, who would never have been ill-at-ease in such a social gathering.

'My family were very disappointed not to meet you today,' the prince told her quietly.

'Whereas here everyone is disappointed that I'm not you—you carry the accolade of being *real* royalty, unlike me,' Ruby retorted, only to bite her lip a few seconds after that hot rejoinder had escaped her for she would have preferred to keep that particular thought to herself.

'You are imagining that. A beautiful woman in fashionable apparel is almost always more welcome than a man,' Raja fielded without skipping a beat.

Wajid introduced them to an older couple, who represented a charity that ran an orphanage just outside Simis, which Ruby, apparently, would be visiting the next day. In the wake of that casual announcement, which was news to Ruby, she appreciated how little freedom she now had when it came to how she might choose to spend her time. Her time evidently now belonged to an ever-growing list of duties, engagements and activities, not least of which was her need to learn the language so that a translator did not have to dog her every footstep.

'You're very quiet. What's wrong?' Raja enquired as Ruby mounted the stairs that led back to her suite.

'It's not important.' Ruby pushed open the door and sped through to the bedroom to change into something more comfortable. A maid was engaged in hanging clothes in a closet there, *male* clothes. Her soft full mouth compressing as she recognised that fact, Ruby walked back into the main reception room where Raja was poised by the window.

'You're staying in this suite with me?'

'Married couples usually share the same accommodation,' Raja pointed out evenly.

Temper roused by that tranquil response skittered up through Ruby in an uneasy rush. He made it sound so simple but their relationship was anything but simple. 'I didn't realise that but for that plane crash you would have married my cousin Bariah,' she admitted. 'I hadn't worked that out yet.'

'A marriage would hardly have been included in the peace accord if the royal families did not have a bride and a groom in mind.'

As usual what Raja said made perfect sense and her teeth gritted in frustration. 'I'm sure you would have preferred a proper Ashuri princess!'

Face deadpan, Raja gazed steadily back at her, patently refusing to be drawn on that touchy topic.

Tension roared through Ruby's rigid stance like a hurricane seeking an outlet. 'I *said*—'

'I am not deaf,' Raja cut in very drily. 'But I do wonder what you expect me to say in reply to such an assumption.'

Flushed and furious, Ruby surveyed him. 'Is an honest answer too much for me to ask for?'

'Not at all, but I will not insult either you or your late cousin with the suggestion that I might compare two completely different women and voice a preference for either,' Raja advanced, eyes cool while his strong jawline set hard as iron. 'That is not a reasonable request.'

'Well, as far as I'm concerned, it's perfectly reasonable!' Ruby slung back heatedly.

'But to answer you would be disrespectful.'

'Unlike you I'm only human. Naturally I want to know although I don't know why I'm bothering to ask. Bariah was a real princess and would've had much more in common with you than I have.'

'No comment,' the prince pronounced stonily and with much bowing and scraping the little maid emerged from the bedroom and left the suite.

'Bariah spoke the language, *knew* this country.' Ruby's statement was pained for after spending only hours in the Ashuri palace she was all too conscious of her deficiencies.

'Given time and patience you will learn,' Raja murmured quietly, his lack of tension merely increasing the adrenalin surge ready to charge through Ruby's veins.

Ruby was in no mood to be comforted. 'My cousin would have known automatically how to behave in every situation—'

'Wajid already thinks you're doing a marvellous job,' Raja imparted gently.

As she stiffened defensively her eyes flared bright as topaz gemstones. 'Don't patronise me!'

'I'm going for a shower,' Raja breathed, casting his jacket down on a chair and striding into the bedroom.

Ruby stilled in her restive stalk round the spacious room and shot a startled glance in his direction as she followed him into the bedroom. 'You're actually planning to sleep in here with me?'

In the act of unbuttoning his shirt, Raja dealt her an impatient glance and said nothing.

For a timeless moment Ruby watched a wedge of masculine torso appear between the parted edges of the shirt. 'There are two big sofas in the room next door,' she pointed out, in case he had not yet noticed the possibility of that option.

Raja treated that reminder to the contempt he evidently felt it deserved. His eyes burned hot gold below his black, spiky lashes, his jaw squared, giving his face a dangerous edge.

'All right…I'll take a sofa,' Ruby pronounced, determined to stick to her guns. It was her belief that if she reinforced their separation they would both soon forget those boundaries they had unwisely crossed and return to their original agreement.

Raja elevated a deeply unimpressed and sardonic black brow and stripped off his boxers to walk fluidly into the bathroom. As nude exits went it scored an impressive ten in the cooler-than-cool stakes. While the shower was running, Ruby made up a bed on a sofa for herself, donned her pyjamas, doused the lights and climbed in. Hermione snuggled in next to her feet.

A little while later, a wild burst of barking drove her from the brink of slumber.

'Call off the dog or I will put her out to the kennels,' Raja growled, his face grim in the light spilling from the bedroom.

Ruby leapt off the sofa, snatched the snarling Hermione up into her arms and attempted to soothe her overexcited pet. 'What are you doing in here?'

'Retrieving my wife,' Raja traded in a wrathful tone of warning.

'I'm not your wife, not your proper wife!' Ruby launched furiously back at him, inflamed by that insistence and the label.

'So you're not a real princess or a proper wife. Then what are you?' Raja challenged impatiently, bending down from his considerable height to haul her up into his arms while she clutched Hermione frantically to her chest. 'My sex buddy? A friend with benefits?'

He then went on to employ a third term of description, which was crude enough to make Ruby's soft, full lips fall open in shock and her big, brown eyes flame. 'How *dare* you?'

Raja settled her down on the bed with a good deal more care than she had grounds to expect from an angry man. Hermione tried to bite him. Composed in the face of that attempted attack, he scooped up the animal and put Ruby's pet out of the room. From the other side of the door Hermione whined and scraped the wood.

'Are you planning to do the same to me if I stand up to you?' Ruby enquired furiously. 'I am not sleeping with you again—'

'I'm not very interested in sleeping right now either.' At least six feet three inches tall and magnificently male, Raja threw back the sheet and slid into bed beside her.

'I am not your sex buddy or that other thing you mentioned!' Ruby proclaimed in a rage.

'No, you're my wife,' Raja repeated again, immovably stubborn on that point.

Ruby was taken aback when he got out of bed again and crossed the room to reach for his jacket and retrieve something from a pocket. He returned to bed and reached for her hand.

'What are you doing?' she demanded apprehensively.

'I'm replacing your wedding ring.' And this time the ring on her finger was a perfect fit as well as being very different from its predecessor. The first ring had been a plain gold band but the second struck her as a good deal more personalised for it was a slender platinum ring chased with ornate decoration.

'Don't call me your wife again,' Ruby muttered helplessly, twirling the ring round her finger with a restless hand. 'It makes me feel trapped.'

This time Raja did not hide his anger. His nostrils flared and his dark golden eyes scorched hers like burning arrows, leaving her feeling alarmingly short of breath. 'You should be proud to be my wife,' he told her without hesitation.

Her breath rattled in her tight throat. She had not meant to insult or offend. Without warning things had become terrifyingly personal. 'I'm sure I would be proud if I loved you,' she whispered in a response intended to soothe.

'Love!' Raja loosed a derisive laugh of disagreement. 'What need have we of that with the fire that burns between us?'

Well, so much for the emotional angle, she was thinking irately, for clearly she had not married a romantic guy, when sure fingers trailed across her cheekbone and captured her chin. His other hand curving to her waist, Raja lowered his proud, dark head and claimed her full, pink mouth hungrily with his. There was a split second when she might have pushed him away and her slim body braced and her hands rose in protest against his broad shoulders to do exactly that. But the moist slide of his tongue between her lips and the hand rising below her pyjama top to curve to the plump swell of her breast sent a flood of damp heat to the tender flesh between her thighs and a surge of such hunger that she shivered in shock. The dark force of desire took her by storm, every fibre of her being sitting up, begging and clawing for more.

# CHAPTER SEVEN

'WE SHOULDN'T do this!' Ruby gasped in a last-ditch attempt to reclaim control of the situation while she mustered sufficient self-discipline to drag her tingling mouth from the unadulterated magnetic allure of his.

Having already whisked her free of her pyjama bottoms, Raja threw back his tousled dark head and angled his lean hips to let her feel the hard evidence of his erection against her stomach. She quivered, fighting her desire for him with all her might, for at that instant desire had as much of a hold on her as a powerful addiction in her bloodstream.

'You mustn't get me pregnant!' Ruby exclaimed in a sudden panic, anxiety gripping her at the thought of suffering such a far-reaching and serious consequence. Just for a moment she could barely credit that she had ever been stupid enough to run that level of risk.

A hand spread below her hips to raise her to him. 'We took no precautions in the desert,' Raja reminded her with a frown.

'But we don't need to run that risk now. I take contraceptive pills but I missed some when we were there so for the rest of the month I need to take extra precautions.'

Raja found it deeply ironic that the potential pregnancy from which she was so keen to protect herself would have been a source of much rejoicing in both their countries. He suppressed that knowledge, for once uninterested in the bigger picture and concentrating on his own reactions for a change. As he studied her stunning oval face with burnished golden eyes of anticipation, he was startled to discover that he was willing to want whatever would make her happy. 'It's OK. Don't worry about it. I will protect you—'

'We can't be sex buddies…it's indecent—'

'I like indecent,' Raja confided huskily, trailing provocative fingertips very gently along the tender skin of her thigh so that she became even more painfully aware of the awesome strength of her own craving. 'In fact I could live beautifully with indecent.'

To silence the argument he sensed brimming on her lips he tasted her sultry pink mouth with the lingering eroticism that came so naturally to him, sensually teasing the soft fullness of her lower lip before penetrating her mouth in a smooth, explicit thrust. And while he kissed her he was skimming the ball of his thumb against the most sensitive spot on her entire body with a shocking expertise that made her stifle a scream while she writhed and gasped her response.

Before she could catch her breath from that onslaught, Raja leant back from her to rip open a foil packet and make use of a condom. Her heart thudded violently up tempo. She would not let herself think about what she was doing. She was rebelling against everything she knew because she had never wanted anything so much as she wanted him in that moment. And without a doubt she was ashamed of it, ashamed of the wild seething longing that controlled her, befuddling her brain and enslaving her body.

Raja sank into her in a long, slow surge, stroking her tender flesh with his. It felt so indescribably good that she cried out and her inner muscles clenched and convulsed around him. In the throes of extreme pleasure, he shuddered violently, as entrapped in that hunger as she was. 'It's never been like this for me before…' he confided.

Or for her, her brain echoed but speech was beyond her. Her whole body was attuned to every movement of his. With every subtle shift of that lean, powerful physique of his the dark pleasure rose in a sweet suffocating tide. He withdrew and then delved deep, moving faster and faster and her spine arched and she moaned in frantic excitement, defenceless against the feverish beat of exquisite sensation. Her climax finally rippled through her in an unstoppable force and she flamed into countless burning pieces before she dropped back to planet earth again. Another cry was dragged from her as the violent tremors of his final pleasure rocked her slight body with renewed sensitivity and sensation.

Raja eased back from her to study her with appreciation. He bent his head to press a kiss to her cheekbone. 'You're amazing,' he told her breathlessly.

'What have we done?' Ruby lamented out loud, already gritting her teeth, aware that in yielding to her hunger for him she had given way to weakness for the first time in her life. And that acknowledgement hurt her pride, really hurt.

Laughing, Raja described what they had done in the most graphic terms and she curled a hand into a fist and struck his shoulder in reproach. 'This is not a joke.'

'You're my wife. We had sex. Our desire was mutual and natural and the slaking of it rather wonderful. Why the fuss?' Raja enquired with a slumberous smile of satisfaction while he marvelled at the unfathomable way in which she drew out the lighter side of his nature.

Ruby was jolted by the reality that he was in a totally different frame of mind and mood. He was celebrating while she was filled with regrets. 'It's not that simple—you know it's not. We made an agreement—'

'A foolish agreement destined to be broken from the outset,' Raja countered without an ounce of uneasiness. 'How could we marry and live in such proximity and not surrender to the attraction between us?'

In rejection of that stance, Ruby twisted free of his arms and rolled away to the far side of the bed. 'That's not what you said to me at the time.'

At that precise reminder, an impatient look skimmed across Raja's face. 'Choice didn't come into it—I had to win your agreement to marry me—'

'*Had* to?' Ruby prompted stiffly, her whole attention lodged to him with unwavering force.

Far from impervious to the threat of the drama waiting in the wings, Raja raked his fingers through the black hair falling into curls at his brow and sent her a look of reproach. 'You are not that naive, Ruby. With this marriage we brought the end to a war and created a framework for a peaceful future for both our countries. There is nothing more important than that and I never pretended otherwise. We sacrificed personal freedom for the greater good.'

That grim little speech, voiced without sentiment, froze Ruby to the marrow and felt like an ice spear thrust through her heart. He had torn any possibility of fluffy illusion from their relationship to insist on showing it to her as it truly was. But had she ever been in doubt of what their relationship entailed? A marriage that was part of a peace treaty between warring countries? A royal husband, who had married her because it was his duty to do so? Exactly when had she begun to imagine that finer feelings might be incorporated in that logical and unemotional package?

Scrambling out of bed because she was hugely uncomfortable with any physical reminder of what had just taken place there, Ruby pulled on her wrap and folded her arms. She would be reasonable, totally reasonable and practical just as he was, she told herself urgently. 'You said that we made a foolish agreement. On what grounds do you base that charge?'

'When we made that agreement, we were already strongly attracted to each other.'

'But you didn't argue that at the time,' Ruby protested.

'Sometimes you can be very naive.' Raja sighed, expelling his breath in a measured hiss and stretching back against the tumbled pillows, a gloriously uninhibited vision of male magnificence. 'Why do you think I went to the UK to meet you? My job was to persuade you to marry me as quickly as possible and assume your rightful place as a royal here in Ashur.'

Ruby lost colour as he made that explanation. 'Your...*job*?'

'There is nothing warm and fuzzy about that peace treaty, Ruby, or the stability that rests on the terms being upheld to the letter of the law. Obviously I was prepared to do pretty much whatever it took to win your agreement,' Raja admitted tautly.

'Obviously,' Ruby repeated, feeling horribly hollow inside as if she had been gutted with a fish knife. 'So, are you saying that you deliberately set out to get me into bed in the desert?'

'I desired you greatly.' Brilliant dark eyes struck challenging sparks off her critical and suspicious scrutiny.

'That's not what I asked you,' Ruby declared. 'I asked you if I was seduced to order, another box to be ticked on your list of duties.'

His clever brow furrowed, his darkly handsome features still and uninformative. 'To order?' he queried huskily.

'Your English is as good as mine, possibly even better!' Ruby snapped, her temper hanging by a fingernail to a cliff edge as she forced herself to seek a clarification that stung her shrinking self like acid. 'Stop faking incomprehension to play for time when I ask an awkward question!'

Unmoved by that indictment, Raja stretched, hard muscle rippling across his broad shoulders and abdomen as he shifted position with the fluidity and grace of a tiger about to spring. 'Is that what I'm doing?' he traded with an indolence she suspected to be entirely deceptive.

Being stonewalled merely aggravated Ruby more and her chin came up, eyes bright with antagonism and resentment now. 'Let me bring this down to the simplest level. Did you or did you not take off your boxers and lie down with me that night for the sake of your precious country?'

Raja very nearly laughed out loud at that demand but restrained the urge, aware it would go down like a lead balloon. 'I am willing to confess that I never had any true intention of allowing our marriage to be a fake. I hoped to make our marriage real from the day of our wedding.'

The barefaced cool with which he made that shattering admission shook Ruby, whose nature was the direct opposite of calculating, to her very depths. 'So, you deceived me.'

'You put me in a position where I could do little else. A divorce between us would be a political and economic disaster. Any goodwill gained by our marriage would be destroyed and offence and enmity would take its place. And how could I continue to rule this country without an Ashuri princess by my side?' he demanded bluntly. 'Your people would not accept me in such a role.'

Unfortunately for him, Ruby was in no mood to recognise the difficulties of his position or to make allowances. Deep hurt allied with a stark sense of humiliation were washing through her slight body in poisonous waves. 'You deceived me,' she said again, her voice brittle with angry bitter condemnation. 'I gave you my trust and you deceived me.'

'I always intended to do whatever it takes to make you happy in our marriage,' Raja breathed in a driven undertone, his dark eyes alight with annoyance and discomfiture, for he was well aware that he had been less than honest with her and that went against the grain with him, as well. 'That is the only justification I can offer you for my behaviour.'

'But if it takes a divorce to make me happy you're going to make it difficult,' Ruby guessed, her face pale and tight with the self-control she was exerting as she turned on her heel. 'I'm sleeping on the sofa tonight.'

As the door eased shut on her quiet exit Raja swore, jolted by a powerful wave of dissatisfaction more biting than any he had ever known. He had wounded her and he had never wanted to do that. Although it would have been very much out of character he badly wanted to unleash his temper and punch walls and shout. But the discipline of a lifetime held, forcing him to stop, think and reason. Pursuing her to continue the altercation in the state of mind she was in would only exacerbate the situation. He had chosen honesty and maybe he should have lied but he believed that the woman he had married deserved the truth from him.

Ironically, Raja believed that he knew what his wife wanted from him. After all, almost every decent woman he had ever spent time with had wanted the same thing from him: eternal devotion and commitment and all the empty words and promises that went along with them.

At a young age Raja had learned to avoid getting involved with that kind of woman. His mistress Chloe's unconcealed greed was a great deal easier to satisfy and the main reason why Raja much preferred relationships based on practicality and mutual convenience.

Ruby, however, was very emotional and she would demand more than he had to offer. Ruby would want things that would make him grossly uncomfortable. He looked back down the years to when he had been a student deeply in love for the one and only time in his life. She would want romance and poetry, handholding and constant attention and if he even looked at another woman she might threaten to kill herself, he recalled with a barely repressed shudder. He was no woman's lapdog and, although his father was a noted poet in Najar, Raja secretly hated poetry. He groaned in increasing frustration. Why were some women so difficult? So highly strung and demanding? Her metaphoric cup was half empty but in comparison his was almost full to overflowing. Ruby was a very beautiful and very entertaining woman and he had just enjoyed the most fantastic sex with her. That was enough for him and an excellent foundation for a royal marriage between strangers. He was more than content with what they already had together. Why couldn't she be content? And how was he to persuade her of the value of his more rational and reserved approach?

On the sofa, which had all the lumps if not the worn appearance of a piece of furniture that had served beyond its time, Ruby tossed and turned. She was stunned that Raja could admit to telling her a barefaced lie. He had agreed to her terms. He had said the words but he hadn't *meant* them. Clearly he had been diametrically opposed to a platonic marriage and the first chance he got to change that status quo he had snatched at it.

Just as Ruby had snatched at Raja out in the desert, craving the hot, hard passion of that lean, strong body against hers! Lust, that was all it could have been, and she had given way to that lust and without much of a struggle. It didn't matter how much she blamed the upsetting circumstances of their kidnapping for what had transpired. In her heart she knew that nothing would ever have happened between them had she not found Raja al-Somari downright irresistible in the flesh.

But it seemed that Raja had made love to her for much more prosaic reasons than mere desire. He had slept with her to consummate their marriage, to make it a *real* marriage and ensure that she was less able to walk away easily. How much did he really find her attractive? Was it even possible that he was the sort of guy who had set out to bring her down simply because she defied his wishes and expectations? How many women had actually said no to Prince Raja with his fabulous looks and even more fabulous wealth? Had she only made herself an irresistible challenge?

Her eyes prickled with stinging tears of humiliation that rolled slowly down her face in the moonlight that filtered through the windows, which had no curtains. She had never had the power to guess what went on in Raja's arrogant, dark head. Their confrontation tonight had been an education. He had been a total mystery to her and a dangerously fascinating one at that, she acknowledged painfully.

Possibly she had been overdue for the experience of meeting a man who affected her more than she affected him. Had she got too full of herself? Too convinced she could not be fooled or hurt by a man? She had assumed she could call the shots with Raja and he had just proved that she could not. The guy she had stupidly married was much colder, more astute and ruthless than she could ever be. Raja had manipulated her into doing what he wanted her to do when she slept with him and in doing so he had crushed Ruby's pride to dust.

Hermione was standing guard over Ruby's sleep when Raja entered the room soon after dawn. With a snarl, the little dog launched herself at him and he caught the animal. He suffered a bite on his arm before he got the frenzied little dog under control and deposited her outside the suite with a word of command to the guards standing outside to take care of her. Raja then strolled quietly back across the room to study his soundly sleeping wife. She didn't take up much space on the sofa and she looked achingly young. Below the tousled mane of blonde hair, only her profile was visible. He could see the silvery tear tracks marking her cheek and he cursed under his breath, his conscience pierced afresh. He had screwed up, he had screwed up royally. He should have kept his mouth shut. Lying didn't come easily to him but the truth had done way too much damage.

Somehow he had to redress that damage and make their marriage work. With no previous experience in the marital department and only a long unhelpful history of unscrupulous mistresses to fall back on, Raja felt unusually weak on the necessary strategy required to make a wife happy. Particularly a wife as unusual as Ruby. An apology would probably be in order. It was not that he had done anything he shouldn't have done, he reasoned in frustration, more a question of accepting that in her eyes he was guilty and that for the sake of better marital relations he had to respond accordingly. He would buy her something as a gift, as well. Flowers? His nostrils flared and he grimaced. Flowers had the same nauseous effect on him as poetry. Diamonds? He had never met a woman who didn't melt when he gave her diamonds…

## CHAPTER EIGHT

FROM her small collection of clothing, Ruby selected a black dress she had bought to wear at her mother's funeral and a beige cotton casual jacket. She would be too warm in the garments but they would have to do because she couldn't wear the red suit again. Some minimal make-up applied to conceal the puffiness of her eyes and her pallor, her hair caught up in a high ponytail for coolness, Ruby forced herself to walk out to the dining area and join Raja for breakfast.

'Good morning…' Raja murmured lazily as if they had not parted at odds the night before.

'Good morning.' One glance at that handsome face and her mouth ran dry and her heart thumped loudly behind her breastbone, while a tiny heated knot of reaction pulled taut in her pelvis and made her clench her thighs together as she took a seat opposite him. Face burning with discomfiture, she suddenly didn't blame herself any more for succumbing to Raja's lethal sex appeal. He was a heartbreakingly beautiful man. Her biggest weakness was her failure to appreciate how clever and calculating he might be, but now that she did know she would be a great deal more cautious.

'I've made arrangements for a new wardrobe to be assembled for you in Najar,' Raja informed her.

'I do need more clothes. I don't own dressy outfits but I wouldn't want anything too expensive or flashy,' Ruby responded thoughtfully as he poured tea for her and she buttered a roll. 'The state this country is in, it wouldn't be appropriate for me to be dressed up like some sort of celebrity.'

'Wajid would disagree with you. He thinks life is too dull here and that you will bring some much-needed colour and the promise that brighter times lie ahead. Here you *are* a celebrity, whether you like it or not, and celebrities dress up.'

Zuhrah joined them along with her male administrative counterpart, Asim, who organised Raja's diary. Ruby's engagements at the orphanage and at a school were discussed and useful sheets of facts tucked into a file for her. She could not help noticing that the heavy-duty visits, like one to a homeless camp and another to a makeshift hospital, fell on Raja's shoulders, Wajid evidently having decided such venues were no place for a lady. A lighter note was struck when a maid appeared with a crystal vase filled with the most exquisite white roses, which she placed on the table.

'Oh, how lovely!' Ruby got to her feet to lean down and draw in the rich opulent perfume of the perfect blooms and only then noticed the gift envelope inscribed with her name. She recognised Raja's distinctive handwriting immediately. Eyes veiling, her facial muscles freezing, she took the card and sat down again to open it with pronounced reluctance.

*I am sorry for upsetting you. Raja*

Her teeth gritted. She reckoned there was never a truer word written than that apt phrase but she was unimpressed by the apology, for a wife barely able to look at him never mind speak to him was naturally a problem he had to fix. No doubt any effort made towards that objective would be all for the greater good and the peace treaty, as well.

'Thank you,' she said with the wooden intonation of a robot and gave him an even more wooden smile purely for the benefit of their audience of staff. Wajid would have been proud of her, she reflected bleakly. Instead of throwing the vase at her royal husband she had smiled at him, showing a restraint in her opinion that raised her near to sainthood. After all, had he been sincerely sorry would he not just have apologised across the table?

Ruby didn't do a good fake smile, Raja acknowledged wryly while he wondered if it had been accidental or deliberate that at one point she had actually pushed the vase of roses out of her way to lay down her file. And then he could not credit that he had actually spared the brain power to wonder about something so trivial! He left the room to phone his jeweller and explain what he wanted: a diamond of the very highest calibre. Raja did not embarrass easily but her silence over breakfast had embarrassed him. He did not want their differences paraded in front of their staff for inevitably it would lead to gossip and the news that their marriage was in trouble would enter the public domain very soon afterwards.

Wajid accompanied Ruby to the orphanage and revealed that Raja had requested that he do so as soon as he had realised that Wajid had scheduled them to make visits separately.

'His Royal Highness is very protective of you,' Wajid told her with approval. 'When he is unable to be with you he wants you to have every possible means of support.'

It occurred to Ruby that that was paradoxical when Raja seemed to have the power to wound her more than anyone else. His protectiveness meant nothing, she reasoned unhappily. The prince was simply one of those very masculine men who deemed a woman to be more helpless and instinctively expected to have to take care of her. That in the desert she had proven him right on that score still blasted a giant hole in her self-esteem. But why did she feel so unhappy? Why had he hurt her as no other man had ever succeeded in doing since her stepfather had gone out of her life?

It hadn't just been sex for her, Ruby conceded reluctantly, striving to be honest about that. Raja was strong and clever and resourceful and she admired those traits. Add in his looks, boundless sex appeal and equally extensive charm and her defensive barriers had begun crumbling so fast she had barely registered the fact. Of course she had never met the equal of Raja al-Somari before. He came from a different world and culture but he had also been shaped by every educational advantage and great wealth and status. Twenty-odd years earlier, Ruby's mother Vanessa had made the mistake of falling in love with just such a man. Was Ruby about to make the same mistake? Not if she could help it.

The limousine in which she was travelling drew up outside the orphanage, a cluster of relatively modern buildings that had mercifully not been targeted by the Najari soldiers. As the older couple she had met at the reception the night before appeared on the steps to welcome them, Ruby had no more time for introspection. She had always loved children. As her visit progressed she was alternately appalled by the scale of loss many of the children had suffered in losing their entire families and then touched by the resilience of their spirits. The orphanage was in dire need of more trained staff, bedding and toys but most of the children were still able to laugh and smile and play.

One little girl attached herself to Ruby almost as soon as she appeared by sliding her tiny hand into hers. About three years old, Leyla had big dark eyes, a tangle of black curls and a thumb firmly lodged in her rosebud mouth.

The orphanage director was surprised by the little girl's behaviour and explained that she was rather withdrawn with the staff. Leyla's parents had died during the war. Unfortunately there was no tradition of adoption in Ashuri society and many people were struggling just to feed their own families. Leyla clinging to her skirt, Ruby spent the most time with the younger children and listened while a story was being told. When the time came for Ruby to leave, Leyla clung to Ruby as if her life depended on it and, lifted from her, wept inconsolably. Ruby was surprised at how difficult she found it to part with Leyla. Just the feel and scent of that warm little body curled trustingly in her arms had made her eyes sting with tears. All of a sudden her own problems seemed to shrink in comparison.

Ignoring Wajid's disapproving expression, Ruby promised to come back and visit in the evening. Their next visit to a temporary school housed in tents was a good deal more brisk but also less formal as Ruby mingled with teenagers and answered their questions as best she could, trying not to wince or stiffen when the court advisor admonished those he considered were being too familiar with his royal companion.

'I don't like formality. I'm more of a hands-on person and that's the only style I'm comfortable with,' Ruby informed the older man as they drove off.

'Royalty should be more reserved,' Wajid preached.

A determined look in her level eyes that Raja would have recognised, Ruby said quietly, 'I'll carry out my engagements as the ordinary person that I am, Wajid. I can only do this kind of thing because I like mingling with people and chatting to them.'

'Princess Bariah would not have dreamt of lifting a crying child,' the older man was reduced to telling her.

'I am not Bariah. I grew up in a different society.'

'One day soon you will be a queen and such familiarity from your subjects would seem disrespectful.'

Aware that a man old enough to be her grandfather was almost certain to cherish a less liberal viewpoint on suitable behaviour, Ruby dropped the subject. But she had not noticed Raja standing on ceremony with their guests at the reception the evening before. He had appeared equally friendly and courteous with everybody.

When she got back to the palace she was so tired she lay down. For quite some time she thought sadly about Leyla. The little girl had touched her heart and she was wishing that there were something she could do to help her before she finally fell asleep for several hours. She wakened when a maid knocked to deliver a garment bag. Unzipping it, she extracted an opulent sapphire-blue evening dress and high-heeled shoes. Her expression thoughtful, she checked the size of both.

Only minutes later, Raja joined her in the bedroom.

'Did you organise this?' she asked, extending the dress.

'Yes. This evening you'll be meeting friends and relatives of your late uncle and his family. You would feel ill-at-ease if you were underdressed in such a gathering,' Raja forecast smoothly.

'You even got my sizes right,' Ruby remarked, thinking how very, very handsome he was, even when in need of a good shave, for dark stubble clearly accentuated the sensual curve of his sculpted mouth. 'You're obviously used to buying clothes for women.'

A slight frown at that remark drawing his ebony brows together, Raja swung fluidly away to remove his jacket and made no response.

But Ruby was not so easily deflected. 'Are you in the habit of buying for your sisters?'

'They do their own shopping,' Raja admitted.

'So, you are accustomed to buying clothes for the

other women in your life,' Ruby gathered, not a bit averse to making him uncomfortable if she could.

'No comment. I'm glad you like the dress.'

Her brown eyes flamed amber. 'Your hide is as tough as steel, isn't it?'

'I never said I was a virgin,' Raja shot back at her with sardonic cool, his strong features taut.

'Oh, I had already worked that out for myself,' Ruby retorted, thinking of how smoothly he had seduced and bedded her.

In retrospect the level of his experience with her sex was obvious to her and to her annoyance that awareness loosed a whole flock of curious questions inside her head. How had she compared to his other lovers? Did he go for blondes, brunettes or redheads or any of the above? Would he even have found her attractive had she not been a long-lost and almost forgotten Ashuri princess? Every question of that ilk that crossed Ruby's mind infuriated her. Why was she letting him make her feel insecure and vulnerable? Now that she knew the truth behind their consummated marriage, she would be better able to protect herself.

'There will not be another woman in my bed while you remain my wife,' Raja volunteered abruptly, his brilliant, dark eyes welded to her expressive face.

'My goodness, do you think I care?' Ruby forced a laugh and then plastered an amused and scornful smile to her lips. 'I couldn't care less what you do. I have to take account of the reality that we're stuck with each other for the foreseeable future so there's no sense in fighting every step of the way.'

'You make a good point,' Raja responded although outrage had shot flames of gold into his gaze when she declared that she didn't care what he did.

'And I'm not asking you to sleep on the sofa tonight and I'm not sleeping on it either. We're adults. I'm asking you to respect that agreement you think is so foolish and forget that we ever had sex.'

Wonderment consumed Raja as she spoke. Forget about the sex? She stood there looking like every fantasy he had ever had in her little black dress with her beautiful eyes, sultry pink mouth and glorious legs tempting him and she thought he could easily return to treating her like a sexless stranger? He *had* deceived her by cloaking his true intentions, he reminded himself fiercely. This was the punishment, the payoff. He had to give her time to adjust to her new role.

'I will do my best,' Raja replied flatly.

He emanated angry vibrations and she wondered why that was. The need to get inside Raja's head and understand what made him tick was, Ruby was discovering, a constant craving. Did he only want to make love to her because he thought that should be his right as a husband? Or would he have wanted her anyway just for herself? And why, when she had never planned to become intimate with him, should that distinction matter to her?

Later he did up the zip on the blue dress and it fit her like a tailor-made glove, the rich colour flattering her fair colouring. As she sat at the dressing table straightening her hair Raja came to her side and handed her a jewellery box. 'It is a small gift.'

Ruby lifted the lid and stared down dumbstruck at the flawless glittering teardrop diamond on a pendant. Small wasn't the right word. It was a *big* diamond and, although she knew next to nothing about the value of jewellery because she had never owned any beyond a wristwatch, she guessed that a diamond that large had to be worth a small fortune.

'Thanks,' she mumbled in shock.

'Allow me.' While she lifted her hair out of the way, Raja clasped the pendant at the nape of her neck. She shivered as his fingertips brushed her sensitive skin and that little knot of sexual hunger in the pit of her stomach tightened up a notch. 'I would've given you earrings but your ears aren't pierced.'

'No, I'm a total unbelievable coward. I once went with a friend and she fainted when they did her ears. She bled all over the place too—it put me right off!' Ruby confided, suddenly desperate to fill the awkward silence.

His shrewd, dark eyes screened in his reflection in the mirror, Raja rested a hand on her taut shoulder. 'Ruby…'

'My mother said my father chose my name, you know,' she volunteered abruptly. 'He said that a virtuous wife was worth more than rubies. It's kind of insulting that the only future he could see for me was as someone's wife.'

'But I am grateful to have you as my wife.'

'Only because I was part of the peace treaty,' Ruby fielded, flatly unimpressed by that declaration. 'Spoils of war and all that.'

* * *

Two weeks later, the night before Ruby's first visit to Najar, Raja was enjoying a pleasant daydream. A century or so earlier had he acquired Ruby as the spoils of war, she would have belonged to him…*utterly.* It was a heady masculine fantasy to toy with while he was being driven to the orphanage that his wife had contrived to visit alone almost every evening since her initial official visit there. He had Wajid to thank for that information, for Ruby had kept very quiet about where she took off to during their rare moments of leisure.

Ruby took care not to share that time with him. It was yet another vote of no confidence from his wife, who was not his wife in any way that mattered, Raja conceded grimly. They might still share the same bed but she had placed a bolster pillow down the middle of it. That had made him laugh the first night, but within a week the comedy aspect had worn very thin.

His cell phone pinged with a message and he checked, frowning as the snap Chloe had put in of herself shone up at him, all blonde hair and a wide, perfect smile. Ruby did not possess that perfection of feature. Her nose turned up at the tip and she had the cutest little gap between her front teeth. Yet whenever he saw Ruby there was no one else in the room capable of commanding his attention. His handsome mouth curled as he read the suggestive text from his mistress. He had no desire to exchange sexy texts. That didn't excite him. Chloe was becoming a liability. On the other hand if Ruby had felt the urge to send him a suggestive text he would have responded with imagination and enthusiasm, he acknowledged with self-derision. Unfortunately there was as much chance of a sext coming from Ruby as of Ashur sending a rocket to the moon.

Raja, however, remained conscious that he had no real grounds for complaint. His bride was already performing her duties as a future queen with considerable grace and good humour. Her naturally warm personality had great appeal. The Ashuri people liked her easy manner and chatty approach, not to mention her frankness in referring to the days when she had led the life of a young working woman.

Forewarned by a call of his impending unofficial visit, the orphanage director greeted him in the hall and took him straight to Ruby. Ruby was in the nursery with a little girl on her lap, painstakingly reading out a few brief words from a picture book in the basic Ashuri language, which she was working so hard to learn. A cluster of children sat on the floor round her feet.

'The princess is a natural with children. It's unfortunate that the child she is holding—Leyla—is becoming a little too attached to your wife,' the older woman told him in a guarded undertone.

Raja got the message intended. He watched the little girl raise a hand to pat Ruby's cheek and then beam adoringly up at her, her other hand clutching possessively at Ruby's top. He watched Ruby look down at the child and realised that he had a problem that cut both ways, for his wife's lovely face softened into a deeply affectionate smile. Raja would have been elated to receive such a smile but he never had. When Ruby saw him in the doorway, she leapt almost guiltily upright, arms locking protectively round the child in her arms.

A staff member approached to take the little girl and Ruby handed her over, visibly troubled when the child began to sob in protest.

'Raja…' Ruby framed in a jerky, almost soundless whisper, for she was so astonished to see him standing there that her voice just deserted her.

Clad in the long off-white tunic called a *thaub* that he wore most days, Raja looked fantastically handsome, the smooth golden planes of his classic masculine features demarcated by the exotic set of his lustrous dark eyes and high cheekbones. Her tummy flipped like a teenager's and she froze, feeling foolish and very much aware that she was hopelessly infatuated with her husband, which was one reason why she avoided his company as much as was humanly possible. He was like an ever-growing fever she was trying to starve into subjection in her bloodstream.

'I had some news I wished to share with you,' Raja imparted lightly. 'Until Wajid mentioned it, I had no idea that this was where you were coming most evenings.'

'I enjoy being with the children. There's no formality here—it's relaxing,' she told him.

'Mrs Baldwin said you're fond of one particular child—'

'Leyla…there's just something about her that grabs my heart every time I see her,' Ruby admitted, opting for honesty. 'I really love spending time with her. She's so sweet and smart.'

Installed in the limo he had arrived in, Ruby said, 'What news wouldn't wait until I got back to the palace?'

'There have been arrests here and in Najar. The members of the royal households who shared our itinerary with the kidnappers have been identified and arrested, as have their supporters.'

Taken by surprise by that information, Ruby frowned and asked, 'Who were they?'

'An aide on my father's staff and a private secretary from Wajid's team here in the palace. Wajid is very ashamed of that link. Be tactful with him if he raises the subject. He is very much aware that the kidnapping could have ended tragically.'

'But we were unhurt,' Ruby hastened to remind him.

Her husband looked grave, his sensual mouth compressing. 'Ruby…tempers run high with memories of the war still so fresh. Fighting could have broken out again. Our lives and those of others were put at risk. The mercenaries whom the perpetrators hired to act for them have fled the country and are unlikely to be apprehended but a prison sentence is inevitable for the citizens involved.'

'I understand.' The justice system was rigid and retribution fell swift and hard on those who broke the laws in their countries. Ruby was already learning to temper her opinions in the light of the society in which she now lived, but it still occasionally annoyed her to depend so much on Raja's interpretation of events and personalities.

Just weeks earlier she had claimed that she intended

to be as much involved as Raja in ruling Ashur and could only marvel at her innocence, for the longer she lived in the palace, the more she appreciated how much she still had to learn about the constantly squabbling local factions and the council of elderly men who stalled and argued more than they made decisions. Raja spent a good deal of his time soothing difficult people and in meetings with the Najari investors financing the rebuilding of Ashur. His duties seemed endless and he was working very long hours because he was also dealing with his duties as Regent of Najar from a distance. Unable to offer much in the way of support, Ruby felt guilty.

Indeed the longer she stayed in Ashur, the more confused and unsure of her own wishes Ruby was becoming. She was fully conscious that Raja had married her with the best of intentions and acted as he saw fit in an effort to turn their platonic marriage into a lasting relationship. He had played the hand he had been given without intending to hurt or humiliate her. He wanted her to stay married to him but to date he had put no pressure on her to do so and she respected him for that. Yet while he was bearing the blame for the dissension between them she knew that she had played a sizeable part in her own downfall by being so violently attracted to him. Her decision to surrender to that attraction had badly muddied the water and her thinking processes and encouraged her to want more from him than he was ever likely to give her. When she had specified and demanded a marriage of convenience, how could she blame him for *her* change of heart?

At the same time avoiding Raja and keeping to the other side of the bolster in the bed was beginning to feel a little childish. She was also living on her nerves because her period was currently overdue. She had told herself that her menstrual cycle could just be acting up. But in her heart of hearts she was terrified that her misfiring cycle combined with the new tenderness of her breasts meant that she had fallen pregnant. She had abandoned all restraint in the desert with Raja and it looked as though she might well be about to pay a price for that recklessness.

'The little girl you were with,' Raja commented quietly.

Instantly, Ruby tensed. 'Leyla? What about her?'

'Have you gone to the orphanage every evening?'

'Have you a problem with that?' Ruby countered defensively.

'The child seems very attached to you. Is that wise?' he prompted gently. 'She will be hurt when you disappear from her life again.'

Annoyance hurtled up through Ruby and she closed her hands together very tightly to control her feelings. 'I have no plans to disappear.'

Sensing her distress at what he had suggested, Raja stretched out a hand to rest it on top of her tensely knotted fingers. 'We're leaving Ashur tomorrow for a couple of weeks. You have many claims on your time now.'

'I…I was thinking of adopting Leyla!' Ruby flung at him, finally putting into words the idea that had been growing at the back of her mind for two weeks and working on her until it began to seem a possibility rather than a wild idea. 'I know you'll probably think I'm crazy but I've become very fond of Leyla. Whatever it takes, I'd very much like to give her a home.'

Astonished by that outspoken admission, Raja studied her. 'But you're planning to divorce me...'

Ruby frowned. 'Well, eventually, yes, *but*—'

'Then I suspect that you have not thought this idea through,' Raja intoned. 'The Ashuri Court of Family Law would not countenance foreign adoption and would wish the child to be raised here where she was born with her own language and people. I doubt that you are willing to offer her that option.'

'I would love her,' Ruby breathed in stark disagreement as the limo drew up outside the side entrance to the palace. 'Leyla needs *love* more than she needs anything else!'

'Love is not always enough,' Raja drawled softly.

In receipt of that hoary old chestnut, Ruby shot him a furious look of disagreement and took the stairs to their suite two at a time. Her heart was hammering like mad behind her breastbone because she was genuinely upset. Having finally got up the courage to voice her hopes with regard to Leyla, she had been shot down in flames. The hard facts Raja had voiced rankled and hurt. Evidently there was no question of her trying to adopt Leyla if she was planning to ultimately divorce Raja. But *was* she planning to divorce him?

Exactly when would she be able to walk away from Raja without that decision impacting on the stability of Ashur? She could not imagine a date even on the horizon when she might leave her marriage without there being a risk of it leading to political upheaval in her late father's country. Her decision to marry Raja had been rash in the extreme, she conceded ruefully. She had not looked into the future. She had failed to recognise that a short-term fix might be almost worse for her country of birth than her refusing outright to marry Raja. A divorce would unleash more political and economic turmoil. Raja was right about that, for she had listened to people talking and seen for herself how much weight rested on their marriage as a symbol of unity and reconciliation. An image of Leyla's tear-stained little face swam before her now and her heart turned over inside her chest.

'What do you know about love?' Ruby demanded, challenging Raja as she poured the mint tea waiting for them on a tray. 'Have you ever been in love?'

'Once was enough,' he admitted sardonically.

Ironically Ruby felt affronted by that admission. He didn't love her but he had fallen for someone else? 'Who was she?'

His lean strong face took on a wry expression. 'Her name was Isabel. We met as students at Oxford. I was besotted with her.' He grimaced, openly inviting her amusement. 'We read poetry and went everywhere together holding hands.'

'People apparently do stuff like that when they're in love,' Ruby remarked stiltedly, well aware that he had never shown any desire to read her a poem or to hold her hand and, as a result, feeling distinctly short-changed rather than amused.

'The romance turned into a nightmare,' Raja confided tight-mouthed, his beautiful dark eyes bleak with recollection. 'She was very jealous and possessive. Everything was a drama with her. If I even spoke to another woman she threw a scene. I was nineteen years old and totally inexperienced with your sex.'

Sipping the mint tea, which she had learned to find refreshing, Ruby was touched by his honesty, for baring his soul did not come naturally to a man accustomed to keeping his own counsel and concealing his feelings. 'At that age you must have found a volatile woman hard to cope with.'

'She threatened to kill herself when I tried to break it off. I stood up to her but she carried through her threat—she *did* take an overdose,' he admitted gravely, acknowledging her wince of sympathy with compressed lips. 'When I said it was a nightmare I wasn't exaggerating. Eventually Isabel's parents put her into a clinic to be treated for depression. It took me a long time to extract myself from my entanglement with her.'

'And of course it put you off what she saw as love,' Ruby conceded thoughtfully, understanding that perfectly, her brown eyes soft as she tried to picture him as a naive teenager spouting poetry and holding hands. 'But Isabel sounds as if she had a very twisted idea of love. It was just your bad luck to meet a woman like that and get burned.'

Raja shrugged a broad shoulder in a fatalistic gesture.

'My mum, though—she got burned twice over,' Ruby volunteered, startling him. 'She lacked good judgement. She just fell in love and believed the man would be perfect. My father married his second wife behind her back and then told Mum he had no choice because he needed a son and she had had to have a hysterectomy after giving birth to me.'

'And the second burning?' Raja queried curiously, for he was already familiar with the first, although he had been given a rather different version.

Ruby grimaced. 'The reason Hermione distrusts men around me—my stepfather, Curtis. He was always trying it on with me—'

'Your stepfather tried to abuse you?' Raja ground out in an appalled tone, black brows drawing together.

Ruby nodded in uneasy confirmation. 'He started bothering me when I was about twelve. By then Mum was going out several nights a week to a part-time job and I was left alone in the house with him.'

Raja was outraged that she had been targeted at such a tender age by a man within her own home where she should have been safe. For the first time he understood what had given Ruby her essentially feisty and independent nature as well as her distrust of his sex. Angry concern in his gaze, Raja was frowning. 'You didn't tell your mother what he was doing, did you?' he guessed. 'Why not?'

'Because it would've broken her heart,' Ruby proffered heavily. 'She adored Curtis and she'd had a bad enough time with my father.'

'Your stepfather never actually managed to touch you?'

'No, but I lived in terror that he would. It was such a relief for me when he walked out on us. He made me very suspicious of men. He also left Mum absolutely broke.' Ruby set down her cup and began to move towards the bedroom.

'Ruby?'

Ruby glanced back at him warily.

'How much do you want to give Leyla a home?'

Ruby paled and contrived to look both very young and very determined. 'I've never wanted anything more...' *Apart from you*, but that was a truth she refused to voice, watching him as he stood there poised, darkly beautiful and dangerous to her every sense and emotion.

'I will make enquiries on our behalf—'

*'Our?'*

'Only a couple could be considered to adopt her. It would have to be a joint application from us both.'

Astonished by that speech, Ruby trembled with emotion. 'Is that an offer?'

Raja surveyed her steadily. 'No, it is my assurance of support in whatever you decide to do.'

And Ruby knew very well what was going unsaid in that statement. A married couple naturally meant a couple planning to stay married. Lashes lowering, she was too enervated to respond and she turned away and went for a shower. Towelling herself dry in the bathroom, she took stock of her situation. She was in love with him. Why not just come clean about that? She was madly, hopelessly in love with Raja al-Somari! Aside from that sense of duty of his, which had hit her pride squarely where it hurt, she liked everything about Raja. His strength, his intelligence, his generosity. His protectiveness, his understanding, his tolerance. He was no longer just a very good-looking, sexy guy, he was the one she had learned to love to distraction even though she had done her utmost to resist his considerable appeal.

The bedroom was empty. But she left the bolster pillow in the foot of the wardrobe where it stayed by day. Tonight she saw no need for a barrier. In fact she was not quite sure which of them had required the restraint imposed by the presence of the bolster the most.

Thirty minutes later, Raja came to bed and the very first thing he noticed was the missing bolster. He slid into the bed in semi-darkness and lay there. There might as well have been a ten-foot wall down the middle of the bed, he reflected wryly. He refused to give her the excuse of believing that there had been any sort of a price attached to his support in the adoption application she was hoping that they would make. He was very much impressed by her commitment to the child, her willingness to become a mother at a young age when so many women would have chosen only to make the most of his unlimited wealth.

Barely a foot away Ruby lay wide awake, as well. She knew that she wanted him quite unbearably. She also knew that suddenly bringing the sex factor back in before other things were sorted out between them would be extremely imprudent but she was still madly hoping that he would take her unspoken invitation.

But the invitation was ignored and it took her a long time to get to sleep. Hours crept past while she thought about Leyla, wondering if they would be allowed to offer the little girl a home and if Raja would learn to love her, as well. She should have discussed the subject more with him. She had to learn how to be half of a couple and wondered why that skill seemed to come so much more naturally to him. It felt as though she had barely slept when she woke up and recalled that this was the day when she would finally meet Raja's family and see Najar for the first time.

# CHAPTER NINE

'WAJID said that adopting an Ashuri child would be a fantastic PR exercise,' Raja revealed with a look of distaste mid-morning the following day as they travelled to the airport for their flight. 'The orphanage director is pleased about our decision because she hopes that our example will encourage people to consider the other children available for adoption.'

'My goodness, you've been busy,' Ruby commented a tad guiltily at his obvious industry with regard to her hopes concerning the little girl. Having woken soon after dawn when Raja always got up, she had felt distinctly nauseous and had returned to bed only to sleep in late and have a rushed breakfast. A stomach upset, she was wondering now that she felt perfectly fine again, or a symptom of a more challenging condition? Could she be pregnant? How soon would she be able to find out? And how could she check discreetly without anyone finding out?

She was startled when the limousine turned in the orphanage gates.

'I think it's time that I met Leyla properly,' Raja announced, recognising her surprise at that change to their itinerary. 'And I believe that you would be glad of the opportunity to see her again before we leave.'

The Baldwins met them on the doorstep to express voluble thanks for the sizeable donation that Raja had made to the orphanage. He had not shared that fact with Ruby and was clearly uncomfortable with the couple's gratitude. They were ushered into an office and Leyla was brought to them there. Her little face lit up when she saw Ruby and she ran in her eagerness to greet her, only to fall to a halt when she saw Raja. He crouched down to a less intimidating height and produced a ball from his pocket. Leyla clutched the ball in a tiny fist while surveying Raja with great suspicion. But Raja was perfectly at home with her, talking to her, smiling and teasing until the child began to giggle and hide her face.

Witnessing that surprising show, Ruby was learning something she hadn't known. 'You're used to kids.'

'I ought to be. My sisters have five children between them and my cousins must have about thirty,' he volunteered, finally standing up with Leyla content to be held in his arms, her thumb stuck in her mouth, her eyes bright.

The effort he was making, the kindness he displayed, Ruby reflected on a tide of quiet appreciation, just made her love him all the more. Suddenly the fact he had taken advantage of her susceptibility to him in the desert no longer mattered and her resentment melted away. Hadn't she encouraged him and taken the final decision? As she had good reason to know he was a very practical and dutiful guy, loyal to his country, his family, faithful to his promises and keen to meet every expectation no matter how unreasonable it might be. And at its most basic, all Raja had ever wanted from her was the willingness to make their marriage work. But the man whom she had resented for that no-nonsense aspiration was also the same one holding the little girl she had come to care for and he was willing for both their sakes to consider making her a part of his illustrious family. And no man Ruby had ever met had been willing to expend even a tenth of Raja's effort and thoughtfulness into making her happy.

Arriving in the country of Najar was not remotely like flying into Ashur. For a start there was a proper airport that was very large and sophisticated. In fact, as Ruby looked out open-mouthed at the busy streets through which they were being driven with a police escort and motorcycle outriders, Najar seemed to have nothing at all in common with Ashur. Towering office blocks, apartment buildings, fancy shopping malls and exotically domed mosques all blended together in a well-designed city with wide, clean streets. She saw at once why Raja had looked at her in disbelief when she had accused him of wanting the throne of Ashur. Her birth country was very much the poor relation, decades behind its rich neighbour in technology and development.

In contrast, the royal palace was still housed in an ancient citadel separated from the aggressively modern city by the huge green public park that stretched outside its extensive walls.

And the palace might be ancient on the outside but,

from the inside, Ruby soon appreciated that Raja's family home bore a closer resemblance to a glossy spread from an exclusive design magazine. The interior was so grand and opulent that she was stunned by the eye-watering expanse of marble flooring and the glimpses of fabulously gilded and furnished rooms. Her steps had slowed and she was fingering the plain dark dress she had chosen to wear with her nervous tension rising to gigantic heights when a door opened and a group of women appeared. And, oh, my goodness, Ruby's sense of being intimidated went into overdrive as shrieks of excitement sounded and high heels clattered across the incredible floor. Ruby and Raja were engulfed by an enthusiastic welcome.

Raja drew her forward in her little black chainstore dress. 'This is Ruby…' and she wanted to kick him for not warning her that the women in his family wore haute couture even in the afternoon. Indeed one look at Raja's female relatives and she felt like the ugly duckling before the swan transformation. All of them were dressed as if they were attending a cocktail party. They sported elaborate hairdos, full make-up, jewel-coloured silks and satins and fantastic jewellery.

They entered the room the women had just vacated on a tide of welcoming chatter and questions. Fortunately everybody seemed to speak at least some English. Children joined their mothers in the crowd surrounding Ruby. There was an incredible amount of noise. Most of the men standing around in the big room attempted to act as though they were not as curious about Raja's bride as their womenfolk were. One tall young man made no such attempt at concealment and he strode across the room to seize her hand and shake it with a formality at odds with his wide grin and assessing eyes. 'Raja said you were even more gorgeous than you looked in your photo and he was right. I'm his brother, Haroun,' he told her cheerfully.

Ruby thought that it was heartening to know that Raja paid her compliments behind her back that he would never have dreamt of making to her face. Was he afraid she might get big-headed? Or did compliments fall under the dubious heading of romance? Or did a woman in a platonic relationship just not qualify for such ego-boosting frills? Haroun looked like a smaller, slighter, younger version of his big brother and he was rather more light-hearted, for he was cracking politically incorrect jokes about Ashur within seconds. Drinks and snacks were served by uniformed staff and Raja's sisters, Amineh and Hadeel, were quick to come and speak to her.

'You are very beautiful,' Hadeel, a tall, shapely woman in her mid-twenties, told her with an admiring smile. 'And a much more suitable match for my brother than your unfortunate cousin.'

'Am I?' Ruby studied her sister-in-law hopefully. 'I never met my cousin so I know nothing about her.'

'Bariah was thirty-seven years old and a widow,' Amineh told her wryly.

'But she was also a very good and well-respected woman,' Hadeel hastened to add, clearly afraid that her sister might have caused offence.

Ruby, however, was just revelling in the promise of

such indiscreet gossip. She had missed that aspect of female companionship and felt that when Raja's sisters were willing to be so frank with her it boded well for her future relationship with them. Learning that Bariah had been eight years older than Raja and had also been married before was something Ruby could have found out for herself from Wajid, but she had been too proud to reveal her curiosity and ask more questions. She met Amineh's and Hadeel's husbands and a whole gaggle of children followed by a long parade of more distant relatives. Everyone was very friendly and welcoming and she was thoroughly relaxed by the time that Raja came to find her. He explained that his father found large family gatherings very tiring and that he was waiting in the next room to meet her in private.

King Ahmed was in a wheelchair and frail in appearance. He had Raja's eyes and white hair and, although he spoke only a few words of English, his quiet smile and the warm clasp of his hand were sufficient to express his acceptance of Ruby as the latest member of his extensive family. Ruby was surprised to learn that Raja had already told his father about Leyla and their plans. The older man was warmly supportive of their intentions and talked at some length about his sadness over the suffering and disruption inflicted on families during the war.

'I didn't realise that you were so close to your father that you would already have told him about Leyla,' Ruby commented on the way back into the party at the end of their audience with the king.

Raja laughed. 'No matter where I am in the world

we talk on the phone every day. I think he would have been very shocked to hear the news about Leyla from anyone else!'

'I wish I'd known my father,' Ruby confided, feeling a slight nauseous lurch in her stomach and tensing slightly, for she had assumed her tummy upset at the start of the day had gone away and she didn't want it revisiting her while she was in company.

Raja paused to look down at her with his dramatic, dark, deep-set eyes. 'The loss was his, Ruby. I fear that you suffered because he and your mother parted on bad terms.'

'Well, after what he did to Mum, naturally they did.'

'The story of your background that I heard suggested that your mother was aware that your father might well take another wife after they were married. It was a lifestyle practised by several of your ancestors over the past hundred years,' Raja told her quietly. 'Perhaps your mother didn't understand what she was getting into when she agreed to marry him.'

'That's very possible…' Ruby focused wide brown eyes on him that were suddenly full of dismay. 'I can't believe I didn't ask you *but*—'

Raja laughed and rested a silencing forefinger against her parted lips. 'No, do not ask me that question, *habibi*. I would be mortally offended. One wife has always been sufficient for the men in my family and the thought of more than one of you is actually quite unnerving.'

'Unnerving? *How?*' Ruby demanded and just at that moment her fractious insides clenched and went to war with her dignity again. Forced to hurry off to the nearest cloakroom, Ruby was so embarrassed by her digestive weakness that her eyes flooded with tears. Her mood was not improved when Raja's sisters insisted on waiting outside the door for her to ensure that she was all right, for she would rather have suffered the sickness without a concerned audience close by.

When the emergency was over, she was ushered into the building that acted as Raja's secluded home within the rambling fortress. He had his own staff, one of whom showed her up a flight of stairs to a superbly decorated bedroom suite. It was a relief to slip off her shoes there and lie down on top of the bed. A drink reputed to soothe a troubled stomach was brought to her and a little while after that as her tension eased and she relaxed she began feeling fine and eventually and surprisingly rather hungry.

A pair of Saluki hounds trotting at his heels, Raja walked in to study her from the foot of the bed. Hermione had accompanied them and the little dog jumped up at the side of the bed to nuzzle her cold nose against Ruby's hand, the Salukis following to make her acquaintance. 'Oh, they're beautiful, Raja!' Ruby exclaimed, leaning out of bed to pat their silky heads. 'Do they belong to you?'

'Yes. Hermione seems to like them well enough. How are you feeling?' Raja asked

'Great now, believe it or not,' she told him with a hesitant smile. 'I'm going to have a shower and then I'd like something to eat. I'm sorry about all the fuss.'

'Are you sure that you're feeling well enough to get up?'

Ruby slid easily off the bed and scolded Hermione for trying to jump up on it. She could not help noticing that Raja's dogs, who had retreated to sit by the door, seemed to be very well trained. 'Very sure.'

'I'll order a meal.'

'Haven't you eaten either?'

'I wanted to see how you were first.'

Ruby checked out the dressing room in search of her wrap and found the closets and drawers were already packed with unfamiliar clothes in her sizes. 'That's some new wardrobe you've bought me!' she called to Raja.

'It won't matter what you wear. You will still outshine every outfit,' Raja responded huskily.

Ruby was surprised by that tribute. A flowing blue negligee set draped over one arm, she emerged from the dressing room to study him, the colour of awareness lighting up her face. Having discarded his traditional robe, he was in the act of changing into designer jeans and a shirt. The fluid grace and strength of that muscular physique of his still had enough impact to take her breath away. It didn't matter how much exposure she had to Raja al-Somari, he still had the power to trip her heartbeat inside her and make her mouth run dry with excitement.

'Shower,' she reminded herself a little awkwardly.

The bathroom was as palatial as the bedroom and the invigorating beat of the water from multi-jets restored her energy levels. She wondered how Raja had tolerated the weak water flow of the old-fashioned shower in their suite of rooms in Ashur. Since her arrival in Najar she had come to realise that he was accustomed to a lifestyle in which every possible modern convenience and luxury was available to ensure the last word in comfort. She admired him for not having uttered a single complaint while he was forced to stay in the palace in Ashur.

When she returned to the bedroom Raja was talking on the phone in Arabic. He glanced up and then stilled to stare, lustrous dark eyes flaming gold at the sight of her. A wealth of blonde hair falling round her lovely face, her slim shapely figure framed by the flowing blue nightwear, she was a picture. With an abstracted final word he concluded his call and pushed the phone into his pocket.

As she met that intense appraisal Ruby's face flushed, her nipples tightening into prominence while a melting sensation of warmth pulsed between her thighs. As he crossed the room, his eyes holding her gaze with a stormy sensuality that filled her with yearning, she was welded to the spot.

Without a word, Raja pushed the tumble of silky blonde hair back from her cheekbone and lowered his head to trace the seam of her closed mouth with his tongue and then pry her lips apart. Fingers stroking her slender neck, he plundered her mouth with a hungry ferocity that blew Ruby away. Staggered by the passion he made no attempt to contain, she angled her head back, snatching in a ragged breath as she looked up at him through her lashes and collided with the smouldering urgency in his stunning eyes. Her tummy flipped. One kiss and she felt as if he had switched a light on inside her, bathing her in warmth and dazzling brilliance.

'I am already so hot and ready for you,' Raja breathed thickly.

Ruby trembled, insanely aware of the surging dampness and the ache at the heart of her body. She was so wound up she couldn't make her throat produce a recognisable sound. But it was also one of those moments when she knew not a shred of doubt about what she wanted to happen next. Her hands lifted of their own volition to unbutton his shirt.

A wolfish smile tilted Raja's handsome mouth. He bent his head to kiss her again with lingering eroticism. 'I will make it so good for you, *aziz*,' he husked in a tone of anticipation that slivered through her like a depth charge of promise.

And the breath rattled in Ruby's tight throat and her knees went weak because she had every faith in his ability to deliver on that score. He would drive her out of her mind with pleasure and she was way past the stage where she could deny either of them what they both needed. She wasn't quite sure when wanting had become a much more demanding *need* and self-denial an impossible challenge. Mesmerised by Raja's raw sensuality, she stretched up to touch his face with delicate fingertips, tracing those slashing angular cheekbones, and those beautiful sculpted lips. She gasped beneath that carnal mouth as it captured hers with delicious masculine savagery. Suddenly, as if her caress had unlocked his self-control to free his elemental passion, he trailed off the peignoir with impatient hands and pushed her back on the bed. Throwing off his shirt, he came down beside her bare-chested.

Breathing shallowly, the level of his hunger for her unhidden, Raja stared down at her. 'I don't know how I've kept my hands off you for so long. It was pure torment.'

As she pushed up on her elbows, feeling marvellously irresistible, Ruby's eyes brightened and she stretched closer to unzip his jeans. The bulge of his arousal made that exercise a challenge and she laughed when he had to help her and then stopped laughing altogether when he drew her hand down to the long, hard length of his erection in an expression of need that was a huge turn-on for her.

She bent her head and took him in her mouth, silky blonde hair brushing his hair-roughened thighs. Watching her, Raja groaned with intense pleasure, knotting his hands in her hair and then finally pulling away at the peak and surprising her.

'Raja...?'

'I want to come inside you,' he told her raggedly. 'And once isn't going to be enough...'

Shivering in reaction to the coiled-tight ache of need in her, Ruby let him move her. Her body was eager and ready, charged by a hunger so strong it made her tremble. He filled her with a single thrust, sinking into her with a power and energy that almost made her pass out with pleasure. She cried out as he lifted her legs onto his shoulders and rose over her to plunge down into her honeyed sheath again and again. Uncontrollable excitement gripped her as he drove her slowly, surely to a delirious climax. At the apex of delight she came apart under him, writhing and sobbing with mindless satisfaction as the wild spasms of pleasure ripped through her in wave after wave. Afterwards he cradled her close, murmuring in his own language, stroking her cheek with caressing fingers while his lustrous eyes studied her with unashamed appreciation.

It was the middle of the night before they ate.

Ruby wakened feeling sick again at dawn and Raja was very insistent on the point that in his opinion it was time for her to see a doctor. He was worried that she had contracted food poisoning. While Ruby lay as still as she could and fought the debilitating waves of nausea Raja made arrangements for a doctor's visit and got dressed.

An hour and a half later, Ruby received the answer to the big question she had been asking herself for more than a week.

'Congratulations,' Dr Sema Mansour pronounced with a wide smile. 'I am honoured to be the doctor to give you such important news.'

Ruby smiled back so hard her facial muscles ached under the strain. 'Please don't tell anyone else,' she urged, although even as she said that she appreciated that it was not a secret that she could hope to keep for long.

'Of course not. It is a confidential matter.' Lifting her doctor's bag, the young female medic, recommended by Princess Hadeel, took her leave.

A light breakfast was served to Ruby in bed and the maid plumped up her pillows first to ensure her comfort. Indeed all the staff involved in her care in the magnificent bedroom displayed a heart-warming level of concern for her welfare. Munching on a piece of roll without much appetite, Ruby stared into space and wondered how Raja would feel once she made her announcement. Last night they had made love and she had felt buoyant at the knowledge that her husband desired her so much.

But starting a family wasn't something they had ever discussed or planned, although he had proved keen to encourage her desire to adopt Leyla.

Ruby had always assumed that some day she would want children. But until she had met Leyla and Mother Nature had turned her broody, she had believed that the family she might ultimately have lay somewhere far into her future. Leyla, however, had stolen into Ruby's heart and she had experienced such a strong longing to be Leyla's new mum that she had been amazed at herself. And now she was carrying Raja's baby. That hadn't taken long, although it was true that they had been very active in that line in the desert. Ruby flushed hotly at the recollection of a night when she had barely slept, indeed had behaved like a sex addict wonderfully well matched with another sex addict. Wretchedly virile fertile man, she thought ruefully and in shock, for there was no denying that a royal baby in the offing would change everything.

In the short term Ruby had been willing to ditch the concept of divorce and future freedom if it meant she could qualify to adopt little Leyla and raise her as her daughter. In spite of that, though, she had still believed somewhere in the back of her mind that there remained a slight possibility that ten years or more down the line she and Raja might be able to separate from each other and lead their own lives without causing too much of a furore within their respective countries. Now with the needs of a second child entering the equation she felt that she had to be a good deal more practical. She had to ask herself if she was willing to subject possibly Leyla and her future child to the rigours of a broken home solely because she wanted a husband who loved her the way she already loved him. Children got attached to their parents living together as a couple. She had seen the heartbreak among school friends when their parents broke up and one parent moved out. Although in many cases there was no alternative to a separation, Ruby felt that she was in a position where she was still lucky enough to have choices to make.

Raja appeared in the doorway, brilliant dark eyes alive with concern, the taut line of his handsome mouth easing with relief when he saw that she was eating. 'It was a stomach upset, probably the result of you being given so much unfamiliar food,' he reasoned. 'Perhaps we should ask one of the chefs to cook English meals for you.'

'No, what we needed was better birth control,' Ruby contradicted, taking tiny sips of tea to moisten her dry mouth while she stared mournfully back at her husband. 'And I'm afraid that ship has sailed.'

Raja was staring fixedly at her, shapely ebony brows quirked, bewilderment stamped in the angles of his strong face. 'Better birth control?'

'We didn't use any in the desert—didn't *have* any to use,' she conceded heavily for so far being pregnant, between the nausea and the sore breasts, was not proving to be a lot of fun. '*And*...you've knocked me up.'

Raja had never bothered to try and imagine how he might hear that he was to become a father for the first time, but had he done so he was certain that not once would the colloquial British phrase 'knocked up' have featured on his dream wife's lips. 'You're...' Shaken by the concept, he had to clear his throat to continue. 'You're *pregnant*?'

'Yes, congratulations, you're a real stud.' Ruby sighed in a tone that would not have encouraged him to celebrate. 'But it's such a shock.'

Raja shifted his proud dark head in agreement. In receipt of her announcement, which had rocked him on his feet, he felt a little light-headed. 'I feel rather foolish,' he admitted wryly. 'This possibility didn't once cross my mind.'

'Me neither—until afterwards. I worried after we were rescued,' Ruby told him ruefully.

'You should have told me that you were concerned. I can't believe it but in the excitement of the situation I overlooked the risk of such a development,' Raja declared gravely.

'That's not like you,' Ruby remarked helplessly, for she always got the feeling that Raja worked everything out to the nth degree and rarely got taken by surprise. 'At the beginning I even suspected that conceiving a child might have been part of the seduction plan. After all, once you got me pregnant it would be harder for me to walk away from our marriage.'

'But not impossible and I wouldn't wish an unwilling mother on any child of mine.' Raja scored impatient fingers through his cropped black hair, his clear, dark golden gaze melding to hers in reproach. 'I am not a Machiavelli. My desire for you was very strong and I acted on it for the most natural of reasons.'

It disturbed Ruby that she could not work out how he felt about her revelation that she was pregnant. She had originally assumed that he would be pleased, which was why she had announced it in that quirky fashion, striving to be cool. But now she was no longer so certain of his reaction because his innate reserve concealed his true reaction from her. 'I bet you that Wajid turns wheelies when he finds out—it's another piece of good PR, isn't it? Three weeks of marriage and I'm pregnant?'

'And you feel even more trapped than you did already,' Raja assumed, his stubborn jaw line clenching, a muscle pulling taut at the edge of his handsome mouth. 'I know you had already decided that you wanted to offer a home to Leyla, but you are very young to take on the responsibility of parenthood—'

'Raja...girls of fourteen were falling pregnant when I was at secondary school. At twenty-one I'm mature enough or I wouldn't have been talking about trying to adopt Leyla,' Ruby argued, feeling insulted and wondering if he considered her immature.

Raja strolled over to the window and looked out at the lush tranquil garden in the courtyard. His lean classic profile was taut. 'I *do* understand how you must feel. Such massive changes in your life are a challenge to cope with. Be honest with yourself and with me—'

Tension made Ruby sit up a little straighter in the bed. 'Honest about what? And how do you feel?'

'I felt incredibly trapped when I knew I had to get married as part of the peace accord,' he admitted without warning, the words escaping him in a low-pitched driven surge. 'I didn't want a wife I didn't choose for myself. My father reminded me that he didn't even meet my mother before he married her but, as I pointed out to him, he was raised in a different world with exactly that expectation. I never dreamt that I would be asked to make an arranged marriage. I had to man up.'

With that confession, which Ruby was quite unprepared to receive at that moment, she felt as though he had driven a knife into her. It shook her that she had been happy to feel like a victim while ignoring the reality that he might have felt equally powerless on his own behalf. *I didn't want a wife I didn't choose for myself.* That one sentence really said all she needed to know. At heart they had always had much more in common than she was prepared to accept. No doubt he had not shared his feelings on the score of their marriage when they first met for fear of influencing her into a negative response. She could understand that. Yet even so, regardless of how she had felt at the beginning, she had adapted, a little voice pointed out in her head—adapted, without even appreciating the fact, to her new position and responsibilities to live a life that was a great deal more demanding but also more interesting than the life she had left behind her in England.

Paradoxically it had wounded Ruby to hear her husband admit that he too had felt trapped when he had learned that he had to marry her. It was a case of very bad timing to learn that truth at the same time as she told him she had already conceived his child. But perhaps once again she was being unfair to him, Ruby reasoned uncertainly, reluctant to come over all dramatic like his first love. After all, how much enthusiasm could she reasonably expect from him? A baby with a woman he didn't love could only feel like another chain to bind him even though he had already agreed to take on Leyla.

Raja sank down on the side of the bed and reached for her hand. 'We will have two children. We will be a family before we have learned how to be a couple.'

'Not how you would have planned it?' Ruby prompted.

'When it comes to us nothing seems to go as planned and who is to say that what we have now is not all the better for that?' Expression reflective, he sounded more as if he was trying to convince her of that possibility than himself. 'I'm accustomed to change and I will handle this, but you have already had so many challenges to overcome in so short a space of time. This is a tough time for you to fall pregnant.'

Ruby was bewildered. 'I—'

'Naturally I feel guilty. I should have been more careful with you,' Raja breathed curtly. 'You have enough to deal with right now without this added responsibility.'

'You still haven't told me how you feel about the baby. Don't you want it?' Ruby queried anxiously.

Raja dealt her an astonished appraisal. 'Of course I want my own child, but not at the cost of your health and emotional well-being.'

'I'll be fine.' Ruby was disappointed that he had said nothing more personal. 'But most of those fancy clothes you bought me aren't likely to fit in a few months.'

'Not a problem. I like buying you things,' Raja volunteered, his thumb rubbing gently over the pulse in her narrow wrist. 'I want you to spend the next couple of days just acclimatising and catching up on your rest.'

Ruby gave him an impish grin. 'No more all-night sex sessions, then?'

Dark colour highlighted his superb bone structure and his eloquent mouth quirked in reluctant appreciation of that sally. 'Oh, Ruby…' he breathed, his hands gathering her slight body up so that he could kiss her with all the devastating expertise that sent her defensive barriers crashing flat like a domino run.

Feeling daring, Ruby pushed the sheet back. 'You could rest with me,' she muttered in an intuitive invitation.

'I have only fifteen minutes to make a meeting on the far side of the city,' Raja groaned, pausing to extract a second driving kiss, his breathing fracturing as he stared down at her with unalloyed hunger before finally springing up again, adjusting the fit of his trousers to accommodate his response to her. 'You're a constant temptation. I'll see you mid-afternoon and we'll go over the adoption papers we need to lodge to apply for Leyla.'

He found her very attractive, Ruby told herself consolingly. It wasn't love, it was lust, but marriages had survived on less. He was taking the advent of an unplanned baby very much in his stride, but then Raja was the sort of guy who typically rose to every challenge. The very worst thing she could do was brood about what they didn't have as opposed to what they did. In time he might almost come to love her out of habit. What was wrong with that? Did she need the poetry and the hand-holding? It would have been much worse had she fallen in love with a man she couldn't have. A man, for example, who belonged to another woman. Here she was safely married to a very handsome, sexy and exciting man and she was still feeling sorry for herself. Why was that? Was she one of those perennially dissatisfied personalities who always wanted more than she could have?

Ruby was dozing when she heard a mobile phone going off somewhere very close to her ear. With a sound of exasperation she lifted her head and focused in surprise on the slim cell phone flashing lights and lying semi-concealed in a fold of the bedding. It was Raja's phone. It must have fallen out of his pocket while he was kissing her. She closed a hand round it and immediately noticed the photo of the gorgeous blonde.

And that was that. Ruby suffered not one moral pang rifling through Raja's phone and discovering that someone called Chloe had sent him a series of suggestive texts in English. Obviously a woman who was a lover, a woman who had shared a bed with him, enjoying all the intimacies and no doubt many more than Ruby had ever had with him. In shock Ruby read the texts again.

The skank, she thought furiously, appalled by the sexy little comments calculated to titillate the average male. Raja's healthy libido did not require stimulation yet he had been receiving those texts ever since they got married. She went through his phone. If he had sent any texts back to Chloe he had clearly had the wit to delete them.

So, who was Chloe and what was Ruby going to do about her? Was she his most recent girlfriend? Why hadn't he told Chloe to leave him alone? Why hadn't he told her that his relationship with her was over? He had promised Ruby that he would be faithful and that there would be no other woman in his life while he was with her. Suddenly the cocoon of shock that had kept Ruby unnaturally calm was cracking right down the middle…

# CHAPTER TEN

DISTRESS flooded Ruby and for a horrible timeless period she was too upset even to think straight. Men had cheated on Ruby before but invariably because she refused to sleep with them and it had never hurt so much that she wanted to scream and sob and rage all at the same time.

Yet she had instinctively trusted Raja—why was that? She peered down at the photo. Chloe was a very beautiful woman. Few men would feel obligated to ditch a woman with Chloe's looks and penchant for provocative texts just because they had made an arranged marriage. Why would Raja award Ruby that amount of loyalty when he didn't love her?

*I felt incredibly trapped. I didn't want a wife I didn't choose for myself.* Today the revelation about the baby had proved such a shock that Raja had at last chosen to be honest with her, sharing what was on his mind and in his heart. All the time that she had subjected him to her bad temper and resentment over the head of their need to marry he had suffered in silence rather than admit that he felt *exactly* the same way. That truth had cut deep. Was Raja planning to keep Chloe in the background of his life while he pretended to be a devoted husband? Was Chloe to be his secret comfort and escape from the exigencies of his royal life and arranged marriage?

The advent of two children was unlikely to lock Raja closer to home and hearth. In all probability children would make him feel more trapped than ever. The demands of a family and all the accompanying domesticity would never be able to compete with the freewheeling appeal of a Chloe, willing to send him sexy texts about what she longed to do to him between the sheets.

Ruby was devastated. She had understood what Raja meant when he had said that they should have had the time to get to know each other as a couple before they considered becoming parents. She also knew that she had literally shot herself in the foot. Tears trickling down her cheeks, Ruby thought about Leyla and yet she knew she could have done nothing different where that little girl was concerned. Her need to give Leyla the love she craved had been overwhelming. But hadn't she railroaded Raja into that commitment with her? She missed the little girl a great deal and could hardly wait for the magical day when she would have the right to take Leyla out of the orphanage and bring her home as her daughter. She had already pictured sharing that special day with Raja but Chloe's texts and the intimate pledges within them might well be much more of an attraction for him.

Having dressed in a denim skirt and tee and slid her bare feet into sandals, Ruby ate a chicken salad in the shaded arbour in the courtyard. Her stomach was mercifully at peace again. It was a beautiful spot with trees, lush greenery and flowers softening the impact of the massive medieval walls that provided a boundary. In the centre water from a tranquil fountain streamed down into a mosaic tiled basin, cooling the temperature. Had she been in a happier mood she would have thought she was in paradise.

She wondered exactly what she was going to say to Raja about those texts. She would have to be blunt and he would have to be honest. How important was Chloe to him? He had to answer that question.

A burst of barking from Hermione warned Ruby that Raja had arrived. Steps sounded on the tiles and Raja appeared, tall and sleek and darkly attractive in a lightweight designer suit.

'I left my phone here?' Lean brown fingers immediately descended on the cell phone lying on the table top and swept it up. 'I've been looking for it. I use my phone for everything…'

Ruby's pensive face tensed. 'I *know*,' she said feelingly. 'I'm going to be totally frank with you—I've read Chloe's texts. Her photo flashed up and I'm afraid I just had to go digging and I'm glad that I did.'

For a split second, Raja was paralysed to the spot, black brows drawing together, lush lashes flying up on disconcerted dark eyes, his dismay unhidden. 'Chloe,' he repeated flatly. 'That's over, done with.'

'If it's over, why was she still texting you as recently as last week?'

Raja was frowning at her. 'Did you read my texts?'

Ruby lifted her chin but her colour was rising. 'We're married. I felt I had the right.'

Faint colour defined his stunning cheekbones. His proud gaze challenged that assumption. 'Even married I am entitled to a certain amount of privacy.'

'Not if you're going to be married to me, you're not. All right—I snooped. But I stand by what I did,' Ruby told him resolutely and without an instant of hesitation. 'It cuts both ways. Everything in my life is open to you.'

His face was impassive. A smouldering silence stretched between them in the hot, still air and during it a servant delivered mint tea and a plate of the tiny decorative cakes that Raja loved to the table. Dry-mouthed, Ruby poured the tea into the cups, her heart beating very fast.

Raja studied her from semi-screened eyes. Without warning a surprising smile curved his beautiful mouth. 'The idea of you reading those texts embarrasses me,' he admitted.

'Receiving that kind of thing *should* embarrass you,' Ruby told him forthrightly, but the ease of his confession and that charismatic smile reduced the worst of her tension, for she could not credit that he could smile like that if there was anything serious going on between him and Chloe.

'My affair with Chloe is over—it was over the moment you and I consummated our marriage,' he added.

'I'm willing to believe that but, if it's over as you say, why was she still sending you texts like that?' Ruby pressed uncomfortably.

'Think about it,' Raja urged wryly. 'From my point

of view, Chloe was a sexual outlet. From hers, my greatest advantage was that I spent a great deal of money on her and she is naturally reluctant to lose that benefit. As I didn't wish to see her again I arranged to pay her a settlement through my lawyer last week. I can only assume that the texts are supposed to tempt me back to her bed. I didn't reply. I thought to reply would only encourage her.'

'She was your mistress,' Ruby remarked uneasily, relieved that no deeper feelings had been involved, but troubled by the obvious truth that he could so efficiently separate sex from emotion. 'That arrangement sounds so…so *cold*.'

'It suited both of us. I didn't want complications or hassle.' Raja shrugged a broad shoulder, his face reflective. 'But now I have you and as long as I have you I have no need of any other woman.'

There was something wonderfully soothing about that statement, voiced as it was with such rock-solid assurance in her ability to replace his sexually sophisticated mistress. The worst of the stress holding Ruby taut drained away.

'I was really upset when I saw those texts,' Ruby admitted reluctantly.

'I regret that you saw them and had reason to doubt my integrity. In that field, you can trust me, Ruby,' he murmured levelly, his sincerity patent. 'I believe in trust and honesty. I would not deceive you with another woman.'

Her eyes stung like mad and she widened them in an effort to keep the tears from overflowing, but some of them escaped, trickling down her cheeks. 'I believe you,' she said in a wobbly voice. 'And I don't know why I'm crying.'

'Hadeel said you might be very emotional over the next few months because of your hormones,' Raja told her, startling her with that forecast and belatedly adding, 'I told her that you were pregnant.'

Ruby was disconcerted by that admission. 'You've told your family already?'

'Only Hadeel, the sister I am closest to, and she will keep our news a secret until we are ready to share it with the rest of the family. It's such exciting news—I could not keep quiet. I *had* to tell someone!' Raja exclaimed, a mixture of apology, appeal and distinct pride in his delivery that touched her heart.

It was the first sign that she had seen that he was genuinely pleased about the baby and a stifled sob escaped her convulsed throat because inexplicably, even though he had set her worst fears to rest, she felt more like having a good cry than ever. 'I don't know what's the m-matter with me.'

Murmuring soothing things, Raja scooped her up in his arms and carried her back indoors, shouldering open the bedroom door to settle her down onto the comfortable bed.

'Do you want me to start sending you texts like that?' Ruby asked him abruptly. 'I mean, I haven't done anything like that before but I'm sure I could learn the knack.'

Raja dealt her a startled look and then he laughed with rich appreciation of that proposal. 'No, thanks for the offer but I can get by without that sort of thing. To be truthful it's not really my style.'

'Honestly?' Ruby pressed anxiously.

'Honestly. I would much rather do it than talk about it, *aziz*,' he husked with considerable amusement gleaming in his lustrous eyes. 'And of course I have to have you to do it with. That goes without saying.'

'Am I really going to be enough for you?'

'Oh, yes,' Raja asserted. 'More than enough.'

'How can you be so sure?'

'You're special and you were from the start. My first introduction to you was a photo of you when you were fourteen. It was taken outside the cathedral in Simis. Wajid had it in his possession—'

'My goodness, you saw that snap? Mum sent it after we came home from that holiday in Ashur when we were turned away from the palace gates,' Ruby explained. 'I think it was her way of saying that we were perfectly happy whether the royal family ignored us or otherwise.'

'I was very impressed with the photo, and when I saw you for real I was stunned by your impact on me and by how much you challenged me,' Raja confided. 'I only had to look at you to want you. I couldn't take my eyes off you.'

'I couldn't take my eyes off you either,' Ruby said. 'But you admitted earlier that you were very resentful of the need for us to marry…'

'The instant I saw my beautiful bride my fate became instantly more bearable,' Raja told her, laughing at the face she pulled. 'Yes, I'm a very predictable guy—I desired you at first glance and I'm afraid that went a long way towards settling my objections to our arranged marriage.'

Ruby frowned, studying him in disbelief. 'That is just so *basic*.'

Raja spread his hands as if to ask her to hold that opinion. 'But then when I was least expecting it I fell in love with you…'

'And then you…*what*?' Ruby gasped, utterly bemused by that declaration.

'At first it was just sexual desire that motivated me and then it was your smile, your strength and your sense of fun that had even more appeal. I fell in love without even realising what was happening to me,' Raja declared, gazing at her with hot golden eyes in which possessiveness was laced with pride. 'All of a sudden you became the most important element in my world.'

'I don't believe you. You said you slept with me in the desert because you wanted to make our marriage a real marriage.'

'I slept with you purely because I wanted you. Any other aspirations which I cherished were secondary to that simple fact,' Raja intoned levelly. 'I'm not too proud to admit that I wanted you any way I could get you. I was very hurt when you said later that you didn't care what I did.'

Ruby was beginning to believe but she wasn't prepared to let him off the hook too easily. 'But there was a seduction plan?'

Raja curled her fingers into his palm. 'I couldn't resist you.'

'I was pretty horrible to you in the desert. I mean, it wasn't your fault that we were there but I behaved as though it was.'

'You were scared and trying not to show it. I understood that.' Raja bent his dark, arrogant head and brushed his sensual mouth very slowly and silkily across her soft pink lips. 'And then you gave me your body and there was nothing I wouldn't have done for you, nothing I wouldn't have forgiven.'

'I thought that night was amazing but it can't have been so special to you.'

'It was, *aziz*.' Raja extracted a deep drugging kiss that made her tremble and look up at him with dazed eyes. 'But I think I fell in love with you when you said over that hotel lunch you walked out on that I would have been equally willing to marry a dancing bear. No other woman would ever have said such a thing to me. Or maybe our defining moment came when you said very ungraciously that you would only drink *bottled* water from now on—'

'Stop teasing me.' Her fingers speared into his thick black hair and she kissed him back with all her heart and soul, the longing he could awaken slivering through her in a piercing arrow of need.

'That second night we spent together was extraordinary. It was our wedding night,' Raja pointed out, his brilliant eyes resting appreciatively on her beautiful face. 'And wonderful.'

'Yes, it was, wasn't it?' Ruby agreed, arching up to taste his mouth again for herself and hauling him back down to her again with greedy hands.

'I thought I would never love a woman again and then I met you and it was a done deal right from the start. I was so resentful of the need to marry you until I actually met you. You got right under my skin. I tried to stay in control but it didn't work. And then after we were rescued you made it clear that you wanted nothing more to do with me. The flowers and the diamonds didn't make much of an impression and that's about all I had in my repertoire. You vanished every evening and only spoke to me when you had to. I'm not used to being ignored.'

'It probably did you the world of good. I felt stupid.' Ruby wrinkled her nose. 'I'd demanded a platonic marriage and then got intimate with you the first chance I got. I didn't know how to behave after that.'

'I lay in that bed every night burning for you.' Raja groaned, his body shuddering against hers in recollection. 'I have never felt so frustrated and yet so aware that I would be putting unfair pressure on you if I made another move.'

'I did need breathing space.' Ruby rubbed her cheek comfortingly against his hand in a belated apology, hating the idea that he had been unhappy, as well. 'I wanted you as well but I had so many other things—like my new royal life—to worry about. I was exhausted and living on my nerves and afraid that it would be a mistake to trust you too much.'

'The greatest mistakes were mine. I was too impatient, too hungry for you.' Raja sighed, discomfiture darkening his beautiful eyes and stamping his features with regret. 'I should never have touched you in that tent. I rushed you into something you weren't ready for and almost lost you in the process.'

'You can't plan stuff like that. I fell in love with you too,' Ruby murmured, looking at him with loving eyes, revelling in the tenderness of his embrace and loving his strength and assurance. 'But I was so scared I was going to get hurt, that I was falling for a guy who would never feel the same way about me.'

'I won't hurt you, *aziz*. You are my beloved and I can only be happy if you are happy with me—'

'Obviously you got over that trapped feeling—'

'I trapped you with me,' Raja pointed out, dropping the mask of his reserve completely. 'I felt so guilty about letting you fall pregnant. That shouldn't have happened. I was selfish, thoughtless. I should have abstained from sex when I couldn't protect you.'

'That night was worth the risk. I would make the same choice again,' Ruby told him, running a caressing hand across the muscular wall of his warm hard torso and smiling with satisfaction when he pushed against her and sought out her mouth again with barely restrained passion.

'Some day I would like to take you back into the desert and show you its wonders.'

'You were enough of a wonder for me,' Ruby countered, in no hurry to recapture the magic of sand and scorpions, before he kissed her breathless and all sensible conversation was forgotten.

'I really do love you,' he told her some time later when they had sated their desire and they lay close and satisfied simply to be together.

'I love you too but words are cheap—you didn't give me the poetry or the hand-holding,' she complained with dancing eyes.

'Not the poetry, please,' he groaned, wincing at the prospect. 'I don't have a literary bone in my body.'

Unconcerned, Ruby squeezed the fingers laced with hers and kissed his stubborn jaw line, loving the scent of his skin. She was very happy and she would settle quite happily for the hand-holding.

# EPILOGUE

A LITTLE less than two years later, Ruby smiled as Leyla told her brother, Hamid, to put away his toys and began showing him how to go about the task.

A lively little girl of five years, Leyla was very protective of her little brother but bossy, as well. For the sake of peace, Hamid toddled across to the toy box on his sturdy little legs and dumped a toy car in it, ignoring the rest of the cars scattered across the rug. Of course, even as a toddler Hamid was accustomed to the reality that servants would cheerfully tidy up after him and go out of their way to fulfil his every need and wish.

Hamid, the heir to the united throne of Najar and Ashur, was treated like the eighth wonder of the world in both palaces. Hamid might easily have become spoilt by overindulgence but Raja was very aware of the potential problem and he was a strict but loving father. With his black curly hair and big dark eyes, Ruby's son was the very image of his father and an energetic child with a quick temper and a wilful streak. Ruby tried not to laugh as Leyla tried to pressure her brother into lifting more cars and he sat down and refused to move another step in silent protest.

Ruby still felt surprised to be the mother of two young children, nor did it seem possible to her that she and Raja had already reached their second wedding anniversary. The two years had flown by, packed with events and precious moments. Leyla's adoption had been a joy. Ruby still remembered the memorable day when she and Raja had collected the little girl from the orphanage and explained that they would now be acting as her mother and father and that she would be living with them from then on. A decree from the throne had made Leyla an honorary princess so that she would not be the odd one out among any siblings born to her adoptive parents. Happily many of the other inmates of the orphanage had also found adoptive homes since then.

Hamid's birth a couple of months later had provided an excuse for huge public celebrations in Najar and Ashur. Their son was the next generation of their ruling family and a very welcome reminder of all that had changed between the two countries. Ashur was no longer a devastated country on the edge of economic meltdown. Slowly but surely the infrastructure had been rebuilt and the unemployment figures had steadily fallen while more liberal laws had encouraged the development of trade and tourism. As the standard of living improved accordingly the Ashuri people had become more content and travel between the two countries had become much more common.

Raja and Ruby enjoyed great popularity. Ruby had never got the chance to have much input into the ruling aspect of their royal roles because soon after Raja's father, King Ahmed's death the previous year elections had been held to pick a government and the monarchy now held more of a constitutional role. Raja had been devastated by the older man's demise and he and Ruby had grown even closer when he shared his grief with her.

Ruby had never even dared to dream that she might be so happy in her marriage. But Raja made her feel incredibly happy and secure. He was wonderfully patient and loving with the children and endlessly supportive of her. Living with Raja, she felt irresistible and very much loved.

Tall, breathtakingly handsome and still very much the focus of his wife's daydreams, Raja appeared in the doorway of the nursery and smiled at Ruby, making her heart lurch in response. 'It's time for us to leave.'

Ruby emerged from her reverie as Hamid and Leyla pelted over to their father and jumped into his arms. Raja hugged the children and then set them down with the suggestion of firmness, nodding to the staff waiting to take over and extending a hand to Ruby to hurry her away.

'Why won't you tell me where we're going?' she pressed as he walked her out of the palace and led her over to the helicopter parked on the landing pad he had had built.

'It's an anniversary surprise,' he told her again.

When she realised that the helicopter was flying over the desert her heart sank a little. A surprise including a tent would not be welcome. As the craft began to land a glimpse of a familiar rock formation made her soft mouth curve down.

Raja sprang out and swung round to assist her out. 'I've organised electric and a bathroom but I'm afraid there's no supermarket,' he teased her.

Ruby blinked in astonishment at the vast tented structure within view. 'What on earth?'

'The sort of desert lifestyle you can enjoy, *habibi*,' Raja pronounced with satisfaction. 'Every convenience and comfort possible has been organised so that we can celebrate our wedding anniversary and remember how we first came together here…'

'That is so romantic.' In the shade of the tent canopy, Ruby turned in the circle of his arms, her eyes tender. She knew that for his sake she was going to pretend to enjoy every moment of the desert sojourn he had arranged for them.

'I would have done this last year but Hamid was so young I knew you wouldn't want to leave him even for a night,' he explained earnestly.

As she entered the main body of the tent Ruby's jaw dropped at the opulence. There was carpet and proper seats and even overhead fans to cool the interior. There was a proper bedroom and when she found the bathroom at the back of the structure she beamed at him in wondering approval. 'You really do know the way to a girl's heart,' she told her husband. 'How the heck did you arrange all this without me finding out about it?'

'With a great deal of ingenuity and secrecy. I've been planning it for weeks,' he confessed, closing his hands over hers to draw her close and kiss her with hungry fervour. 'Happy anniversary, Your Majesty. May we enjoy many many more together…'

Gazing up into his brilliant dark golden eyes, Ruby felt dizzy with love and longing and thought with a little inner quiver of bathing naked in the cliffside pool with him later. She knew her demand for a bathroom had persuaded him that she wouldn't wish to revisit that particular experience but she was already planning to surprise him with her contrariness.

'I love you so much,' Raja breathed huskily.

'You were going to get all your favourite food for dinner tonight—now you're going to miss out—'

'No, we won't. We have a chef coming in a few hours to take care of our evening meal,' Raja whispered.

'You think of absolutely everything.' Ruby was entranced and she leant up against his lean, muscular chest, listening to the solid reassuring thump of his heartbeat. 'That's one of the reasons I love you. You cross every t and dot every i—'

Tipping up her chin, Raja sealed his mouth to hers and the world spun dizzily on its axis for Ruby. He swept her up in his arms and carried her through to the comfortable bed awaiting them. Happiness bubbling through her, she made the most of his passion, which was only another one of the many reasons why she loved him to distraction.

* * * * *

## ROMANCE

| | |
|---|---|
| **Jewel in His Crown** | Lynne Graham |
| **The Man Every Woman Wants** | Miranda Lee |
| **Once a Ferrara Wife...** | Sarah Morgan |
| **Not Fit for a King?** | Jane Porter |
| **In Bed with a Stranger** | India Grey |
| **In a Storm of Scandal** | Kim Lawrence |
| **The Call of the Desert** | Abby Green |
| **Playing His Dangerous Game** | Tina Duncan |
| **How to Win the Dating War** | Aimee Carson |
| **Interview with the Daredevil** | Nicola Marsh |
| **Snowbound with Her Hero** | Rebecca Winters |
| **The Playboy's Gift** | Teresa Carpenter |
| **The Tycoon Who Healed Her Heart** | Melissa James |
| **Firefighter Under the Mistletoe** | Melissa McClone |
| **Flirting with Italian** | Liz Fielding |
| **The Inconvenient Laws of Attraction** | Trish Wylie |
| **The Night Before Christmas** | Alison Roberts |
| **Once a Good Girl...** | Wendy S. Marcus |

## HISTORICAL

| | |
|---|---|
| **The Disappearing Duchess** | Anne Herries |
| **Improper Miss Darling** | Gail Whitiker |
| **Beauty and the Scarred Hero** | Emily May |
| **Butterfly Swords** | Jeannie Lin |

## MEDICAL ROMANCE™

| | |
|---|---|
| **New Doc in Town** | Meredith Webber |
| **Orphan Under the Christmas Tree** | Meredith Webber |
| **Surgeon in a Wedding Dress** | Sue MacKay |
| **The Boy Who Made Them Love Again** | Scarlet Wilson |

Mills & Boon® Large Print
December 2011

## ROMANCE

| | |
|---|---|
| **Bride for Real** | Lynne Graham |
| **From Dirt to Diamonds** | Julia James |
| **The Thorn in His Side** | Kim Lawrence |
| **Fiancée for One Night** | Trish Morey |
| **Australia's Maverick Millionaire** | Margaret Way |
| **Rescued by the Brooding Tycoon** | Lucy Gordon |
| **Swept Off Her Stilettos** | Fiona Harper |
| **Mr Right There All Along** | Jackie Braun |

## HISTORICAL

| | |
|---|---|
| **Ravished by the Rake** | Louise Allen |
| **The Rake of Hollowhurst Castle** | Elizabeth Beacon |
| **Bought for the Harem** | Anne Herries |
| **Slave Princess** | Juliet Landon |

## MEDICAL ROMANCE™

| | |
|---|---|
| **Flirting with the Society Doctor** | Janice Lynn |
| **When One Night Isn't Enough** | Wendy S. Marcus |
| **Melting the Argentine Doctor's Heart** | Meredith Webber |
| **Small Town Marriage Miracle** | Jennifer Taylor |
| **St Piran's: Prince on the Children's Ward** | Sarah Morgan |
| **Harry St Clair: Rogue or Doctor?** | Fiona McArthur |

1111 GEN STD LP

# Mills & Boon® Hardback

## January 2012

## ROMANCE

|  |  |
|---|---|
| **The Man Who Risked It All** | Michelle Reid |
| **The Sheikh's Undoing** | Sharon Kendrick |
| **The End of her Innocence** | Sara Craven |
| **The Talk of Hollywood** | Carole Mortimer |
| **Secrets of Castillo del Arco** | Trish Morey |
| **Hajar's Hidden Legacy** | Maisey Yates |
| **Untouched by His Diamonds** | Lucy Ellis |
| **The Secret Sinclair** | Cathy Williams |
| **First Time Lucky?** | Natalie Anderson |
| **Say It With Diamonds** | Lucy King |
| **Master of the Outback** | Margaret Way |
| **The Reluctant Princess** | Raye Morgan |
| **Daring to Date the Boss** | Barbara Wallace |
| **Their Miracle Twins** | Nikki Logan |
| **Runaway Bride** | Barbara Hannay |
| **We'll Always Have Paris** | Jessica Hart |
| **Heart Surgeon, Hero...Husband?** | Susan Carlisle |
| **Doctor's Guide to Dating in the Jungle** | Tina Beckett |

## HISTORICAL

|  |  |
|---|---|
| **The Mysterious Lord Marlowe** | Anne Herries |
| **Marrying the Royal Marine** | Carla Kelly |
| **A Most Unladylike Adventure** | Elizabeth Beacon |
| **Seduced by Her Highland Warrior** | Michelle Willingham |

## MEDICAL

|  |  |
|---|---|
| **The Boss She Can't Resist** | Lucy Clark |
| **Dr Langley: Protector or Playboy?** | Joanna Neil |
| **Daredevil and Dr Kate** | Leah Martyn |
| **Spring Proposal in Swallowbrook** | Abigail Gordon |

1211 GEN STD HB

# ROMANCE

| | |
|---|---|
| **The Kanellis Scandal** | Michelle Reid |
| **Monarch of the Sands** | Sharon Kendrick |
| **One Night in the Orient** | Robyn Donald |
| **His Poor Little Rich Girl** | Melanie Milburne |
| **From Daredevil to Devoted Daddy** | Barbara McMahon |
| **Little Cowgirl Needs a Mum** | Patricia Thayer |
| **To Wed a Rancher** | Myrna Mackenzie |
| **The Secret Princess** | Jessica Hart |

# HISTORICAL

| | |
|---|---|
| **Seduced by the Scoundrel** | Louise Allen |
| **Unmasking the Duke's Mistress** | Margaret McPhee |
| **To Catch a Husband...** | Sarah Mallory |
| **The Highlander's Redemption** | Marguerite Kaye |

# MEDICAL

| | |
|---|---|
| **The Playboy of Harley Street** | Anne Fraser |
| **Doctor on the Red Carpet** | Anne Fraser |
| **Just One Last Night...** | Amy Andrews |
| **Suddenly Single Sophie** | Leonie Knight |
| **The Doctor & the Runaway Heiress** | Marion Lennox |
| **The Surgeon She Never Forgot** | Melanie Milburne |

1211 GEN STD LP

*Mills & Boon® Online*

Discover more romance at
**www.millsandboon.co.uk**

- **FREE** online reads
- **Books** up to one month before shops
- **Browse our books** before you buy

*...and much more!*

**For exclusive competitions and instant updates:**

Like us on **facebook.com/romancehq**

Follow us on **twitter.com/millsandboonuk**

Join us on **community.millsandboon.co.uk**

*Visit us Online*

Sign up for our FREE eNewsletter at
**www.millsandboon.co.uk**

WEB/M&B/RTL4/HB